CHASING THE BEATLES

For Grown-up Girls Who Remember

Randi Barrow

ISBN: 1494819597
ISBN 13: 9781494819590
Library of Congress Control Number: 2013923767
CreateSpace Independent Publishing Platform
North Charleston, South Carolina

For my Dad

who made it happen

Table of Contents

Prologue

"Bring me something that will make me laugh." That was my cousin Bridget's only request. She might as well have asked me if I'd invite Tom Hanks along to cheer her up, or Annie Liebovitz for a few quick Polaroids.

I hadn't been able to smile, much less laugh, since Bridget was diagnosed with breast cancer. She, on the other hand, had bravely packed her bags and flown from Los Angeles to Chicago, where she was able to receive her chemotherapy while she slept, claiming it caused fewer side effects, and made you need less of it.

She was about to have the fifth of six treatments. Her husband and daughter had been with her for the first four; now it was my turn. There was something special about my bond with Bridget. Our moms were identical twins, now happy eighty-nine-year-olds still living in the houses next door to each other where we'd grown up. Bridget and I might not have been twins, technically speaking, but we felt like it in our hearts.

Now she faced a challenge I didn't have to face, and asked only that I bring her something that would make her laugh.

"How about a joke book?" my husband offered. I looked at him like he'd told me to bring her a Whoopee cushion. My mom suggested a collection of Marx Brothers movies. Not bad, but not right.

I knew what Bridget meant, and it had nothing to do with the giggles. She was telling me to bring her something that would strike the fear out of her heart. She'd asked me to toss her a lifeline.

The day before I was scheduled to fly to Chicago, I sat in my office at UCLA grading papers. It was a bad time for me to leave. I was overwhelmed with work, teaching four classes this winter instead of the normal two. I glanced at the calendar on my desk: my flight left early the next morning, February 9. For a week I'd been fretting about how to fulfill Bridget's wish. When I saw the date, I suddenly knew.

***

Six hours later, tired, nervous, not yet packed, I stood in the middle of our two-car garage, the one filled with the sealed-up memories of our lives, the one a car had never entered since we moved in twenty years ago. I knew there were boxes that had never been unpacked, because I was looking for the contents of one of them. For the last hour and a half, I'd rifled through filing cabinets, plastic bins, and aging cardboard boxes. It had to be here. Unless it was lost in the move, it was here. Hiding. Somewhere.

I sat down on a sagging pile of file boxes ready to weep. *Think, Annie,* I commanded myself. *Make a connection. It would be packed with* . . . I kept drawing a blank . . . *because that would be the most logical place for it*. With my college stuff? No. High school memorabilia? Already looked. Letters? Unlikely, but I was getting desperate. I jumped up, removed three boxes that sat on top of one labeled "misc. and letts," brushed away the dust and dead bugs, and opened it.

There it was: my first book. Well, manuscript more accurately. The one I'd written about our adventures in the summer of 1964. That's why the date February 9 had jolted me out of my cluelessness. It was the night the Beatles first performed on *The Ed Sullivan Show*, a night that changed our lives forever. The letter I'd written to the publisher sat exposed on top, its envelope long gone. I picked up the yellowed onionskin stationery that I'd thought so sophisticated at the time and read:

Simon and Schuster
Publishers Incorporated December 22, 1964
1230 Avenue of the Americas
New York City, New York

Dear Mr. Simon and Mr. Schuster,

I have enclosed for your professional consideration a manuscript I hope you will like. It tells the story of two fifteen-year-old girls and their practically relentless quest to see the Beatles at their first concert in Los Angeles, California, at the world-famous Hollywood Bowl. The concert is sold out, you see, and so they do everything in their power to find two tickets.

The stuff they do is funny, and sometimes sad, and even includes their slightly weird parents. If either of you have daughters, you should let them read it. They would understand, and they could explain it to you.

I won't tell you the ending, because it would spoil it. This book is based on a true story that my cousin Bridget and I actually lived just last summer. If you decide to publish it, I will change the names to protect the innocent.

Thank you for your time in reading what I hope is my first book, CHASING THE BEATLES, by Annie Street.

Yours very sincerely,
Annie Street

At the bottom of my letter, which was returned along with the manuscript a month later, someone had written just two words in pencil: "No thanks." Even all these years later, it stung a little to see those words. They'd help push me out of my dream of being a writer, and put me on the path to being an English professor, the one with several manuscripts tucked away that she was going to finish as soon as she had some time. No matter.

I lifted the ancient manuscript out of its hiding place and held it like the treasure it was. This was what I needed to bring to Bridget. This is what would make the blood flow in her veins again. This is what would make her remember what it felt like to be fully alive, to be transformed by the power of music, and to believe in what the future held.

Hold on, Bridget, I'm coming. I'm on my way. And I'm bringing the Beatles with me.

APRIL

1964

CHAPTER ONE

All I've Got to Do

First I heard the scream. It came out of the house next door, across their driveway, over ours, and through the bathroom window where I was soaking in a bubble bath of Calgon Bouquet.

I sat up straight, alert. It was the scream of my best friend and cousin, Bridget O'Malley. Not bothering to wash the bubbles off I got out of the bath, and swung a towel around me, gripping it together at the top. Leaving a trail of wet footprints, I walked as fast as I could out of the bathroom, down the hall, past my room, through the kitchen where my Mother sat reading the Sunday paper, and straight for the front door.

It blew in like a hurricane. There stood Bridget, all five-foot-eight of her, a look on her face like she'd seen a ghost walk in and wish her good morning. She held a newspaper up in the air with her left hand and shook it. "They're coming!" she shouted.

"Who? Who's coming?" I could feel a puddle forming around my feet on the old wood floor. My hair clung like tentacles to my back and shoulders.

"The Beatles!"

In unison we took deep breaths, covered our mouths with our hands, and screamed like we were being murdered. She dropped her paper, I dropped my towel. It was the first time anyone had seen me naked since my parents stopped giving me baths, but I didn't care. The Beatles were coming to Los Angeles.

"Annie Street!" my Mother yelled from the kitchen. "Put some clothes on for God's sake, and stop parading around in your birthday suit!"

"Where?" I asked breathlessly, bending down to pick up my towel.

"Hollywood Bowl. In August." Bridget was practically panting in her excitement.

"How much?"

She dropped to the floor, and half sitting, half laying tore through the paper until she came to the ad for the concert. "Five dollars and fifty cents to eight-fifty."

"That means we can go!" I practically collapsed next to her, dazed, thrilled. "What's the number? Let's call right now."

Bridget stuck her face so close to the page her nose touched it. "It's 718-1921."

"718-1921," I chanted, walking quickly back to my room, Bridget close behind, "718-1921." My parents had given me a Princess phone a year earlier as a reward for receiving my first and only report card with straight A's. Its existence ensured that I would never again have enough time to study for such high marks. Thank God. I pushed the buttons carefully, not wanting to risk the delay of dialing a wrong number.

"Hollywood Bowl," a girl answered, sounding as if she'd just stuck her thumb with a safety pin.

"Yes, hello. I want to buy two tickets to the Beatles concert on . . . when is it, Bridget?"

"The 23rd."

"The 23rd of August."

The girl made a snorting sound. "Oh, really? No kidding?"

"Yes. No kidding. I want two tickets, please. Do I come in in person, or do you mail them to me?" I made a frowning face at Bridget to let her know what a jerk the girl was being. She sat across from me on the other twin bed, watching my every move, stretching out her hands as if to say, "What's going on?"

"You're too late. They're all sold out."

"How can they be? It's only April!"

"They sold out in an hour. And please don't cry and scream and tell me you're the Beatles biggest fan because I've heard it about a thousand times already!" She was yelling by the time she finished.

"The least you could do is be nice about it! We *are* the Beatles' biggest fans, and . . . and this is terrible! How are we going to get tickets to see them?"

Bridget was repeating almost everything I said, only she already had tears in her eyes when she whispered, "How are we going to get to see them?"

"You're not. We're sold out. And don't call again, 'cause I'll recognize your voice." She hung up on me.

I pulled the receiver away from my ear and looked over at poor, bleary-eyed Bridget. "They're out of tickets. We don't get to go." I spoke the words like I couldn't grasp them, which I kind of couldn't.

She sniffed loudly. "We have to go. We have to be there."

I felt a chill, sitting there on my bed, with wet hair and towel, in the damp spot I'd made on the pink spread. "We have to go," I repeated, loud and defiantly. "We have to go. There's got to be a way."

Bridget nodded nervously in agreement. "Uh-huh, uh-huh. So . . . how?"

I readjusted the soggy towel around me. "There's got to be a way."

"I heard that part. I was waiting for the 'how' part."

"OK. Go home, give me ten minutes to get dressed, and I'll come over. We won't stop talking till we've figured it out."

"Promise?"

"Of course I promise."

"It's just that it's the most important thing in the whole world to me, and if they're right here, and I can't see them I—"

"Bridget! When the Beatles walk on stage at the Hollywood Bowl, we will be in the audience."

"I mean, I would just die!" She stood up, and sort of shook her coiled mane of dark hair at me like I'd personally denied her the tickets.

"Tell your grandma to start praying to Saint Jude."

Bridget was halfway out the door when she turned back. "But he's the patron saint of hopeless causes. I thought you said—"

"It's just for good luck, you know, while I work on the plan."

CHAPTER TWO

It Won't Be Long

Bridget lay on her bed staring straight up, where a picture of Paul McCartney taped to the ceiling smiled back at her.

"This Boy" played softly on the record player. She sang along with three of the Beatles about how she wouldn't mind the pain.

"Hi, Bridg," I said, sitting on the corner of the bed.

"It's OK," she said listlessly, "you can lay on the other bed." I made myself comfortable on the twin bed across from her. "John's bed" we called it, because his picture was taped to the ceiling on that side. I was never troubled by decisions like Bridget had to face each night—John or Paul? Paul or John? Numerous pictures of all four Beatles were taped above both beds in my room, allowing my imagination to run free.

"I feel so betrayed," Bridget moaned, rolling over on her side so she could look at me.

"By who?"

"By the Beatles. By life." Only John could see me roll my eyes. "This Boy" ended, and the next cut, "It Won't Be Long" started. "It won't be long?" Ha! Right. It's like even the Beatles are mocking us."

"OK, that's it." I got up and lifted the needle off the record. "That's all the feeling sorry for ourselves we're going to do."

"I'm not feeling sorry for myself. My heart is broken. If I move, it will fall out of my chest and get blood everywhere."

"Come on, sit up. OK," I said, sounding like a football coach or something, "what's our goal? To see the Beatles. Let's think of three other ways we can get into that concert besides buying tickets ourselves."

"We could be lowered down on a rope by a helicopter . . ."

"I don't mean a literal way of getting in. Like, for example, someone could give us tickets."

Bridget snorted. "Like who? Santa Claus?"

"No, I mean like a boy could ask us on a date, and he would have tickets."

"Which of the short, pimple-faced boys at St. Boniface would most likely have tickets, Annie? Not one, because they're total dorks. And if they were going to ask someone to go with them, it wouldn't be one of us."

"Michelle Brennan," I said.

"She's not going to ask us because she's a girl. Duh."

"I'm thinking about her dad. Remember? He's some kind of record company guy or something."

"Oh!" Bridget leapt to her feet. "Yes, yes. Didn't he work with, uh, uh . . ." She snapped her fingers trying to remember.

"Trini Lopez."

"Yes! 'If I Had a Hammer.' That was such a bitchin' song."

"See? You're getting the idea. Maybe we could get tickets from Michelle's dad."

"Ahhh!" she squealed in delight. "Let's think of more ways."

I walked back and forth in her crowded room, with its green and white shamrock wallpaper, thinking, observing everything from the stacks of Beatles bubble gum cards, to the stuffed animals, from the record player, with 45s and albums scattered all around it, to the radio. The radio. "Turn it on!" I exclaimed, pointing. "Turn on KHJ. I bet you anything one of the DJs is giving away tickets."

Bridget tripped over her own feet rushing to get to the radio. She tuned in just as an ad for Clearasil was ending. Out of the speaker came the deep and sonorous voice of Mike the

Magnificent, or Mike the Mag as he was known. "How was that for great? Miss Petula Clark right here in our own 93 KHJ studio. It doesn't get any better than that. Or does it?" He paused, which is saying something, because those guys don't even leave spaces between the words.

Bridget and I moved closer to the radio. "OK, kids. This is it. We've been telling you boss boys and girls all weekend here at KHJ about our big ticket giveaway. But you didn't know who, and you didn't know where, and you didn't know when. I'm going to play you three hits in a row—uninterrupted—because when I come back you're going to meet, right here with me on 93 KHJ, Mr. Scottie Pinkus!"

"Scottie Pinkus?" we repeated. Who the heck was he?

"Here with us exclusively, Mr. Scottie Pinkus, manager of the Hollywood Bowl. So let's get started, because when we come back we'll be giving away . . . TEN tickets to TEN of you boss listeners to see THE BEATLES at the Hollywood Bowl!" And with that, the guitar riff of "Sugar Shack" cranked into gear. But you could barely hear it above the screams of two fifteen-year-old girls jumping up and down with happiness.

CHAPTER THREE

Misery

My house and Bridget's were not only next door to each other, they were mirror images. The two driveways ran parallel, with no fence in between, which created a wide, open area. Both of us had bedrooms at the back of the house with windows that looked out on the backyard, and the driveway. So we could call across to each other, and we did, all the time. Today's plan was a little different.

"It will give us double the chance to win if we're both calling," I suggested. "Let's each run our telephones out the window and call from the driveway—the cords are long enough. And we'll both sit out there and call the station till we win."

Bridget was shivering with excitement. "Stand outside my window, and I'll hand you my phone, then I'll do the same for you." I ran outside, and was soon stretching my arms up to receive Bridget's phone. I pulled it as close as it would go to my house, then ran in my front door to do the same with my phone.

"Hi, Annie!" my Dad greeted me. My dad was known as the kind of man who was always smiling, always in a good mood. He sat at his Hammond organ, which was the centerpiece of our living room. "Sure you don't want to go with me today? I don't go on till four." He smiled as his feet played the long wooden pedals, and each of his hands played on a separate keyboard.

"Thanks Dad, I'm busy." I ran to my bedroom to get my phone and to escape the strains of "Sheik of Araby." Every

Sunday my father played the organ for an hour and a half at the El Capitan Theater in Hollywood, one of the old, fancy movie palaces. It was the very definition of torture to listen to a souped-up version of "Danny Boy" or "Bésame Mucho" on the Mighty Wurlitzer. Bridget called it a pukefest, and swore she'd never go again after the one time I made her come with me.

Bridget was waiting at my window; I handed her the pink Princess phone, then grabbed my transistor radio so we could listen while we called. I slipped out the back door just as my dad launched into a fast and furious version of "Stars and Stripes Forever."

"Ready?" Bridget asked, settling in on the warm cement.

"Ready." I was as taut and poised as a swimmer waiting for the starting gun.

Mike the Mag made good on his promise. "We've been telling you about this all weekend, and now the moment has arrived." There was the sound of a drum roll in the background. "Scottie Pinkus is with us. Say something, Scottie."

"The Beatles are coming!" he yelled, so loud and close to the microphone you could barely understand him.

"That's right. The home of Beatlemania '64 is right here, at 93 KHJ. Tell me, Scottie, how many tickets do we have to give away to our listeners today?"

"Ten big ones."

"And where will the lucky winners be seeing the Beatles from?"

"Front row center." We squealed and laughed. I was so excited, I fell sideways and knocked my phone off the hook.

"Get it! Get it!" Bridget cried. I had it back in its cradle in seconds.

"OK, boys and girls, this is it. It's time for Mike the Mag to give you the chance of a lifetime to see the one . . . the only . . . BEATLES!" Noisemakers of every kind sounded behind him. "Are you ready?" he asked, lowering his voice. "Get your pen and paper." That's when I sort of panicked. What if I forgot the number? Or didn't hear it right? Mike the Mag reassured me quickly.

"Now, we want this to be fair, so I'm going to give you the number, make sure you have it, and then Scottie and I are going to count down from ten to one. When I say "one," start dialing if you want to see the magnificent BEATLES!" He and Scottie whooped it up. "The number is 929-4141. Got that? 929-4141. Get your dialing fingers ready. We'll be playing a record while you make your calls, so here we go. Ready, Scottie?"

"Ready."

Their voices were hushed as they counted down, "ten, nine, eight." Then they got louder, "seven, six, five." I had the receiver in my hand, my finger holding the switch down so I could dial fast. "Four, three, two." They waited a full ten seconds before they screamed, "ONE!!!"

We started dialing. 929-4141. Busy. I pushed the button down till I got a dial tone. 929-4141. Busy. I dialed again, yelling, "Did you get it, Bridg?"

"Yes, it's busy."

"Me, too. Keep trying. 929-4141. Busy. I could feel a heaviness building in my heart. 929-4141. 929-4141. Busy, busy, busy. "Love Me Do" played while we frantically tried to win two of those ten tickets. Paul's last, "Oh, oh, love me do," faded, along with John's plaintive harmonica. I dialed, and dialed, and dialed again.

"No," I moaned, "go through!" I hit the buttons hard. "Please go through." I glanced over at Bridget; she was doing exactly the same thing. Her eyes came up to meet mine, and in that moment, I knew it wasn't going to be us.

Mike the Mag was talking again. "Oh, my God, the lines have been jammed! Thank you to all our boss listeners. I think we have our winners, but stay right there because you never know. Maybe someone got disconnected, and it will be your turn to win."

I put the receiver back in its place as he introduced his first winner. "Hi, who's this?"

She was panting, and squeaky. “Hi. It’s Joann. From West L.A.”

“Well, you’re a winner, Joann from West L.A.!” She screamed, of course. I hated her guts.

“So, what do you have to say to Mike the Mag now?”

“I can’t believe it! You’re more than magnificent, Mike, you’re . . . *magnificatious!* You’re *magnificado!* You’re—”

I turned off my radio. “Malodorous.”

“Malevolent,” Bridget responded.

“Malformed.”

“Malarial.”

“Malignant. I’m never listening to KHJ again.”

Bridget sighed. “I guess it’s time for Plan B.”

“That was Plan B.”

“What’s Plan C?”

I shrugged, so sad my face felt frozen. “Just think of all those lucky people who work there. Bridget!” I exclaimed, jumping to my feet. “That’s it! All we have to do is get jobs at the Hollywood Bowl, and we can see them!”

She gasped, her mouth hanging open. “Do you think they’d hire us?”

“Yes! Absolutely.”

“But we’re not sixteen yet.”

“They don’t have to know that.”

“Won’t they make us show IDs or something?”

“We’ll just say we forgot them.”

“Yeah!”

“This is it. I told you when the Beatles walk onstage at the Hollywood Bowl, we’re going to be in the audience. Even if we’re ushers.”

“And . . . and maybe this means we could get backstage . . . and meet them!”

“I’m glad we didn’t win those stupid tickets. This will be so much better.”

CHAPTER FOUR

No Reply

Sister Ignatius was that rarest of creature, a truly sweet-natured nun. She was old and forgetful, almost blind, and practically deaf. That made her a perfect fit for our Wednesday afternoon study hall. It was held in a moldy basement room connected to the so-called cafeteria. They didn't have a real cafeteria at St. Boniface because then we might actually enjoy our food, which would inevitably lead to sin and eternal damnation.

The machines in the cafeteria held only tuna sandwiches, in case you got hungry on a Friday when that was all you could eat. The combination of the moldy smell from study hall and the tuna smell from the cafeteria invigorated us once we discovered the Beatles.

"I'll bet this is just how England smells," Bridget whispered to me, inhaling deeply. "Cold, damp, and fishy."

"Did you talk to Michelle Brennan yet?" I whispered back.

"No, she's up in the front by Sister Ignatius."

"Why don't you go talk to Ignatius, and I'll tell Michelle to come to the back."

"What am I going to talk to her about?"

"Anything. Let's go." We walked up one of the three aisles. I stopped next to Michelle, and Bridget continued on to the front desk.

"Sister," I heard her say, "I was wondering, could you clarify for me the difference between the joyful and the glorious mysteries of the rosary?"

I knelt down next to Michelle. "Can I talk to you for a minute? In the back?" She glanced at Sister Ignatius, nodded her head, and followed me. She slipped into Bridget's seat directly in front of me, and turned around so we could talk. I knew we wouldn't be disturbing the other girls. They were either reading magazines or paperbacks, which put them on that same road to eternal damnation I mentioned earlier. It was getting to be a seriously crowded highway.

"Michelle," I said, "I'll just ask you this directly. And I hope you won't think I'm using you, because we've known each other since—"

"You want Beatles tickets," she said matter-of-factly.

I was shocked. "How did you know?"

She shrugged. "I can put you on the list."

"What list?"

"The list of girls who've already asked me."

I looked around furtively. "There are others?"

"Just about everybody."

"So that means there are a lot of girls ahead of us."

"And boys."

"The boys asked you, too?" I couldn't believe it. Half of our school was male, but they were safely stashed away in another building with separate teachers.

She nodded. "I've told everybody, I can probably get two or three, but that's all. My dad says it's almost impossible."

"That means really only one ticket, right? Because you'll use one, and you'll bring a friend, and then if there's a third ticket, you'll have to choose from all the people who've asked you."

"Pretty much."

"Do you think it would be Bridget or me?"

"Probably not," she answered frankly. "I mean, a lot of people have asked. A lot."

"Yeah," I murmured, watching Bridget coming down the narrow aisle toward us. "Maybe you should do a drawing, like put all the names in a hat or something."

"I'll probably just decide," she answered, getting up to give Bridget her seat back. "And besides, don't you guys want to go together? Would one of you go and leave the other one at home?"

"No!" Bridget and I exclaimed in unison.

"It's both of us, or neither one of us," I added, not having considered the possibility that only one of us would get a ticket.

"Put us on the list anyway," I called out in a loud whisper as Michelle made her way back to her seat.

"A list," Bridget said. "That doesn't sound good."

I shook my head. "Let's stick with Plan C. Saturday we go to the Hollywood Bowl and apply for work. Until then, try to think of a Plan D. Just in case."

"Are you guys talking about the Beatles?" Karen Novak asked us from two aisles over, looking up from her copy of *Dr. No*. We nodded, and glanced at Sister Ignatius to make sure she was still deaf and blind.

"I heard that in England, they let all the people who are crippled or in wheelchairs be put in the first row at the concert. They don't have to buy tickets or anything."

"But we're not crippled," Bridget explained patiently.

"You could pretend to be, and—" she snapped her fingers, "you're in."

"We were thinking we should try to get a job at the..."

"Bridget!" I said so loud half the class turned to look at us. "Let's give some thought to what Karen said." Karen smiled, and went back to *Dr. No*, like she was glad to have been of help.

"Bridget," I hissed. "Don't tell anybody about working at the Hollywood Bowl, or they'll steal the idea."

"Oh, God," she said, looking around, "I'm sorry."

"And I'm not dressing up like a cripple, so this has to work."

"It will," she assured me.

"Because if it doesn't . . ."
"You'll think of something else."
"What makes you so sure?"
"John, Paul, George, and Ringo."

MAY

CHAPTER FIVE

When I Get Home

On Friday nights, my family ate dinner at Bridget's house; on Sundays, they came to our house to eat. Maybe I forgot to mention that our moms are twins, identical twins. They still did everything together, and sometimes I wondered why either of them bothered to get married and have kids.

Bridget's dad, Thomas, owned The Shamrock, the Irish and Scottish shop in downtown Santa Monica. His grandfather was born in Ireland, but Thomas had never been there himself. The way he acted and sounded, you'd think he was fresh off the boat from Dublin. Bridget worked at the shop after school occasionally, mostly because she thought it was hilarious to watch men try on kilts.

That Friday night, Thomas sat in a winged-back chair smoking a pipe, with a blue plaid Tam o' Shanter on his head, gazing thoughtfully at my father. "The wives say they've got a surprise for us." There was the roll of a brogue on his tongue.

"Yes," my dad said from the seat of their little spinet. He played chords softly, no particular song in mind. "I hope they're not going to start dressing alike again." He smiled. "I had a hard time telling them apart."

"Beautiful lassies they are."

I glanced at Bridget, who was rolling her eyes and sticking out her tongue like she was going to throw up. "Grown women shouldn't dress alike, because it's weird and freakish, not because you can't tell them apart."

I could always tell which one was my mom, even though I agreed with Bridget. "It's freakish."

"We'll see soon enough," Thomas said, hitting his pipe lightly against an ashtray, and stuffing it with more tobacco.

"What's for dinner tonight, Thomas? Haggis?" My dad made the same joke every week.

"No, I couldn't find a sheep's stomach in time for dinner." The supposed hilarity of this joke made them both laugh loudly. "Some chicken, I should think. Potatoes, of course. We Irish can't live without our potatoes."

"I could live without them at every single meal of my entire life." Bridget said brightly.

"Mustn't forget where you come from," her dad answered patiently.

"I was born in Van Nuys, California. You're from Wisconsin." A version of this conversation arose often between Bridget and her dad. She wanted him to be normal, and he wanted to give her the romance of a heritage.

Before he could launch into his speech about tradition, her mom called out loudly from down the hall. "Are you ready?"

"Ready," we all answered, with four very different levels of enthusiasm.

"OK, here we come!"

They ran down the hall, and came to a standstill in the middle of the room, shaking blue and gold pompoms. They made cheering sounds like you'd hear from the grandstand at a football game. They wore matching plaid skirts, white cardigan letterman's sweaters, and black and white saddle shoes. I was horrified, maybe even scared.

"What are you doing?" Bridget cried. "Are you OK?"

"What's all this?" Thomas asked, looking amused.

My father, as in love with my mother as the day he met her, stood up, looking enraptured. "Joyce Street, you look beautiful. And Felicia—*bravo!*"

Thomas even put down his pipe, and stood up to get a better look.

"Can you guess?" my mother asked flirtatiously, standing in profile, and holding one pompom high, and one low.

"You're going to a women's prison where you don't care what you look like?" I offered.

"Don't be silly, Annie. Try again."

Her sister started singing an ancient fight song in a low voice. My mother joined her on the second line:

We're U—C—L—A
And we're here to win today
Kick it through the goal post
Seven more points
Bye Bye SC
Cry like a baby
Call your mama
And tell her you lost
To U—C—L—A
The mighty Bruins won today
U—C—L—A
We're number one!

Then they leaped in the air in unison and hollered. My mom kind of held her lower back for a minute afterward like she'd hurt herself. The men applauded, and my dad even whistled. I moved over next to Bridget, all hunched over like I was protecting myself from an attack.

"Can you guess yet?" my mom asked.

"It's easy," Felicia said.

"You're going to a costume party," my dad said, admiring them.

"No, it's more than that," Thomas said, as if only a genius would have figured that out.

"What do you girls think? Can you guess?" Aunt Felicia asked.

"Does it have something to do with a vitamin imbalance in the brain?" Bridget wanted to know.

"No!" her mom scoffed. "Can't you see? We're going back to school!"

I sighed in relief, and felt the terror you feel when grown-ups act weird draining out of me.

"Wow!" my dad said. "Well . . . that's great."

Thomas looked confused. "You're going back to what kind of school?"

"UCLA!" the twins answered, in unison.

"But you two are so . . ." I could tell Bridget didn't want to finish the sentence.

"Old?" her mom cut in. "UCLA doesn't think so." As weirded out as I was, this was kind of interesting.

"How did this happen?" I asked.

The twins looked at each other conspiratorially. My mother answered for the both of them. "We didn't want to get anybody's hopes up, so we did it in secret."

"Did what?" Thomas asked.

"Applied to go back to UCLA," his wife answered. "You know we've always wanted to go back and finish. Not that it wasn't worth dropping out to marry you." She trotted over and kissed him quickly, and returned to stand next to her sister.

"And they accepted you?" I was confounded. They were thirty-seven years old!

"We start in June for the summer semester." My mother looked so proud, and my Aunt Felicia looked, well, exactly the same.

"I'm ecstatic," my dad said. I think there were tears in his eyes. "You've always done so much for us. Now it's your turn." He hugged her, and she put her pompoms around him.

Bridget and I looked at each other like two ornery cats. What would this mean for our lives? More chores? Less supervision? Records never played above a whisper?

"We're very happy for you," I said to the sisters, although volunteering for years of study was something I couldn't quite comprehend.

"Ahhh," my Aunt Felicia sighed happily. "Let me slip out of this getup and put dinner on the table."

"Oh, ah . . ." I began awkwardly. This was the perfect time to ask, when everyone was in a good mood. "Bridget and I got an assignment at school. We have to go to a Los Angeles landmark and then write a paper about it." I hadn't cleared the cover story yet with Bridget, so she looked confused. "And we were assigned to go to the Hollywood Bowl."

"On your own?" my mom asked. "That's a little far."

"I looked at a map, and got a bus schedule and everything. It'll be easy."

"If you can wait till Sunday, you can come with me to the El Capitan, and I can take you over there after I play the morning show. It's just a few miles."

Bridget gasped. "No, no, that's OK."

"Yeah, we have to do it right away, in fact, tomorrow. So . . . we'll be leaving early, and we'll need bus money, and some lunch money."

Thomas dropped back in his chair. "Kids nowadays," he said with a laugh. "In Ireland you'd walk, and bring a potato with you for lunch."

"It's almost fourteen miles away. Twenty-eight round trip!" I said as convincingly as I could, in case my dad thought we should take the walk-and-potato route.

"It will be good experience for you," my mom said, as she headed out of the living room to change her clothes. "Prepare you for the rigors of college."

"That's what I was thinking," I agreed. "Dad, can you spare five dollars?"

He nodded and reached into his back pocket for his wallet.

Bridget's dad did the same, but he was much cheaper than my dad. "I'll be expecting some change, my lass," he said.

"Thanks Dad. I'll eat French fries for lunch. They're made from potatoes."

"So I've heard," he answered, handing her a five-dollar bill.

Our mothers had inadvertently opened the door for our big adventure when they announced their own. Before their little show, I thought our chances of being allowed to go so far on the bus alone were fifty-fifty, to say nothing of getting them to pay for it.

That night, after carefully slipping the five-dollar bill into my wallet, I gazed up at the pictures of the Fab Four on the ceiling above my bed. "Don't worry, boys," I said out loud. "We won't let you down. We're going to be there on August 23rd one way or another."

CHAPTER SIX

Do You Want to Know a Secret

We caught the bus at 7 a.m. on a sunny Saturday morning. "Did you really talk to somebody at the Hollywood Bowl?" Bridget asked, opening a window.

"Uh-huh," I said, taking a bite from the cheese sandwich I'd brought with me for breakfast. "They said to come in and fill out an application and take a test."

"What kind of test?" Bridget popped an orange section into her mouth.

I shrugged. "I didn't ask. I'm more worried about getting there by ten. They said they only see applicants on Saturday mornings."

The bus stopped to pick up passengers, but after the door closed behind them, the bus driver left his seat and came over and stood looking down at us. "Enjoying your meal ladies?"

"Yes, sir," we said.

"Well, there's no eating on the bus. So you can either put it away, or I can let you off here."

"Sorry, we forgot. We'll put it away," I said. "And could you tell us when you get to Highland Avenue?"

"If you want me to tell you when we've arrived at your stop, you have to sit up front near me."

"Thanks," Bridget said. "Come on, let's go up there. I don't want to miss it."

If I'd known it would take almost an hour and a half to get to Highland, I would have stayed in the back and eaten my breakfast all bent over when the driver wasn't looking. It was past 8:30 when we finally stumbled off the bus, tired and hungry.

"Eat fast," Bridget instructed me as we sat down on the bus bench to wait for our next bus. We pulled what was left of our food out of our purses. "The driver said the bus we want comes in five minutes." It lumbered in on time, but with standing room only. An entire hour elapsed before we made it to our next stop, and from there it was a quarter of a mile walk to the Bowl.

"We've got to make it there by ten," I said, waiting nervously for the long red light at Franklin Avenue to change. We raced across, and in a slow run made it to the entrance of the Hollywood Bowl by 9:45. From there we followed pathways that zigzagged across the property, all of them uphill.

Breathless, and not sure where to go, we finally found a maintenance man who steered us in the right direction. Entering the door marked "Employees Only," we were told that the group was meeting out in front of the bandstand that morning. It was almost ten, and we ran all the way.

The band shell covers a stage that looks out at almost eighteen thousand seats built into the Hollywood Hills; the seats and benches seem to go up endlessly. In the open area in front of the stage were about fifty people, all girls. We rushed to join them.

"What if we do get a job here?" I asked Bridget as we ran. "That would be almost six hours on the bus each day."

"Only until August," she reminded me, "and worth every minute."

"All right. That should be it," one of the young men addressing the group said, glancing at his associate. "We're getting groups this size every Saturday now. We're so glad you think enough of the Hollywood Bowl you want to work here. Welcome!"

I stole a glance at Bridget. She was staring at the empty stage where the Beatles would play, where we'd see them for the first time. I stared too, imagining them in their trim suits, their hair shining, bowing low at the end of the performance. What would they play, I wondered? Would I be able to hear them above the screams? Would they be able to see me?

Bridget's elbow jolted me out of my reverie. "Raise your hand."

"Why?" I whispered, raising it high.

"They just asked who's over sixteen."

"As you can see," the young man pointed out, "the Bowl is very large, the terrain is challenging, and it can be difficult to find your way at the nighttime concerts. The only lights are the flashlights carried by the ushers, and our other staff members." I looked around as the group nodded in collective understanding; I was scrutinizing them for telltale signs of Beatlemania. I wanted to know if we had competition. There was nothing as obvious as a T-shirt, or Beatles tennis shoes. I searched for something more subtle: a Beatles watch perhaps, or even a colorless jacket like the Beatles favored. Nothing. Although it did seem weird that there were no boys applying for jobs. I turned my attention back to the speaker.

"Many of you asked what kind of test is expected of you. Today you're going to find out." He bent down and pulled a thin piece of dark fabric out of a box at his feet, and a flashlight out of another box. "The atmosphere before a concert at the Hollywood Bowl is a kind of controlled chaos. Our job is to make sure the control is stronger than the chaos."

His partner took over. "Picture this: It's five minutes to eight, it's dark, patrons can't find their seats, they're worried about being late or missing even a minute of their favorite artist. Or, worse yet, the concert has started, and you're trying to help someone find his seat; other people are annoyed at being disrupted while the music's playing. All the patrons are depending on you to fix it—quickly, and quietly. And there are ten more waiting for you when you're finished with the one you just helped!"

He swung the piece of black fabric around on his index finger and added, "So, this is what your test consists of: Each of you will be blindfolded, and given a flashlight. Don't worry, you can see through the fabric, but it simulates the darkness you'll be working in if you're hired by the Hollywood Bowl. You'll also be given a seating chart with twelve red dots on it. You will have five minutes to find those seats, take the token that is taped to the seat or bench to show that you've found it, and bring it back here."

"Five minutes, that's it," his associate emphasized. "I want you all to come up here and get a blindfold and a flashlight, and a seating chart. When everyone's ready, we'll begin, and the clock will start running."

"Piece of cake," I told Bridget. "Just be sure you run everywhere."

"I'd do it blindfolded and naked if it means I'll be here on the 23rd."

"I'm sure the other applicants would find that disturbing. Save it for the night of the Beatles concert."

"When we'll be here!" she whispered dramatically.

"When we'll be here," I confirmed. "Let's show the other girls how it's done."

We got our blindfolds, flashlights, and seating charts. I did a last quick assessment of the layout before I tied the cloth across my eyes. There were four aisles that went from the front to the back, and seven aisles that cut through them and divided the space into large sections. Assuming they went alphabetically and in a normal numerical sequence, how hard could it be?

"Don't mess up," Bridget said, tying her blindfold. "Oh, my God. I'm blind!"

I quickly tied mine, and had the same sensation. I couldn't see a thing. "How are we supposed to find the seats?" I asked her, as I fumbled to turn on my flashlight. "Hey Bridget—you can see the chart a little if you turn on the flashlight." I started waving it around in front of me to see what else I could see. Turns out I couldn't see the first or the second girl I bumped into, or the fact that I was headed toward the stage instead of the seats.

One of the men who'd spoken to us grabbed my arm. "Not that way; you'll land in the pool," he said, referring to the ten-foot-wide pool that separated the stage from the first row of box seats. "It takes a few minutes for your eyes to get used to it."

"All right, ladies," one of them called, clapping his hands. "Are we about ready to go?" A few voices cried out for him to wait. "I'll give you fifteen more seconds, and it's ready or not, here we go."

Girls murmured, and fussed, and made a lot of noise in their efforts to get ready.

"On the count of three, I want you to go to the seats indicated on your seating charts, get the tokens taped there, and return to us at the stage within five minutes. You may not take off your blindfolds until you have turned in your tokens to one of us. If you do take your blindfolds off, I'm sorry to say we will have to discard your application. Are we ready?"

"Ready," most of us responded.

"All right, then—GO!"

My desire to win my place as a Hollywood Bowl employee propelled me straight up the stairs toward section P1. The incline was deceptively steep. I guess it had to be if almost eighteen thousand people were going to fit in there. I kept my flashlight in front of me to light the way, but I was almost completely blind, seeing just enough not to trip over the concrete steps as I made my way up and to the right. If I wanted to see what row I'd reached, I had to stop and find the small letter indicator.

I was already winded when I reached section P1. The urge to lift my blindfold was almost irresistible. Shining the flashlight on the seating chart, I found the tiny dot that indicated the exact seat I needed: number 17. I rushed down the aisle, which wasn't difficult as the seats were long benches. "Where are the numbers?" I mumbled, searching in vain for them. I found them by feeling with my hands. They were on the very top of the bench, aimed up at the sky. I was at seat number 42.

At least a minute had elapsed, and I had eleven more tokens to find, assuming I found number 17. It was still almost as dark as when I put the blindfold on, but I ran anyway. "Oh," I cried, as I saw number 21. Four seats later I was looking frantically for the token. It wasn't on the seat, or the ground, or next to the seat number. I got on my knees—there it was—taped under the seat amid a sea of previously chewed gum. I grabbed it; the scotch tape gave way easily.

"Whoo-hooo!" I shouted. OK, where next? Section Q2. All the way on the other side. The closest access aisle that criss-crossed the sections wasn't far away, and I hustled as fast as I could to find it. I was nearing Q2 when a body seemed to come out of nowhere, and slammed into me, knocking me off my feet. My hand went up automatically to lift off my blindfold, but I caught myself just before I did it. "Are you OK?" I asked the girl I could barely see. She stifled a sob.

"I think maybe I broke something."

"What?" I was incredulous, and wanted so desperately to be on my way.

"My arm."

"Well, can you . . . just take your blindfold off and call to one of those guys?"

Her voice was choked with tears when she answered, "But if I do, I'll never get to see the Beatles." The seconds were ticking away. I knew then, with certainty, that I'd never get eleven more tokens and be down in front before our five minutes was up.

I pushed my blindfold up over my head. "Where are you hurt?" I asked, squinting in the bright sun, looking at a slight, young girl sprawled across the cement aisle.

"It doesn't matter if I'm hurt. I can't stop!" she cried. "I have to see them."

"I think you're going to have to figure out another way to do it."

She sat up, slowly pushing her blindfold to her forehead, sniffling and emitting little sounds of frustration. "Come on, let's get you some help," I said, looking down toward the stage. The two men were laughing so hard, one of them was bent over, hands on his knees. The other was practically holding his sides.

"Hey!" I shouted. "We need some help up here!" I guess the sound of their own laughter prevented them from hearing me. The other girls were still blindfolded, except for one who was racing from place to place as if somehow it wouldn't be noticed that she broke the rules. I thought I saw Bridget in a side area down by the stage, wandering around with one arm out in front of her like you might see at a game of Pin the Tail on the Donkey.

"Do you really think it's broken?" I asked the girl I'd bumped into as I helped her to her feet.

"Probably not. I'm just so disappointed. Me and my girlfriend thought that if we got jobs here we could see the Beatles when they play in August." She glanced at me with a look that was something between defensiveness and mild embarrassment.

"Oh? Are they playing the Bowl?" I asked, still not wanting to admit our reason for being there was the same as hers.

"Yeah. This is my third time trying to pass this test."

"What's the most tokens you've ever gotten?"

"Three."

"Has anybody ever gotten them all?"

"No."

"Then why do they do it like this?"

"Because they know everybody's here so they can get to see the Beatles."

"Do you think that's true?"

"Of course it's true. And that's why you're here too, even if you won't admit it. We're the unlucky ones. We don't have family or friends that could pull strings or whatever to get tickets."

"I'm not one of the unlucky ones," I said sharply. "I'm going to be there when they play."

"That's what every other girl out there is thinking." She gestured toward the pitiful group of blindfolded girls just as one of the men on the stage blew a whistle, letting us know time was up.

"There are other ways."

"Like what?" She looked at me with a kind of desperation I found uncomfortably familiar.

"Well . . ." She leaned on me with her uninjured arm as we walked down the endless steps toward the front. "They have to arrive somewhere," I continued, "and they have to stay at a hotel, and eat at restaurants, and maybe visit with friends . . ."

"True, you might get to see them. But none of that will get you into the concert, will it?"

"I'm going to be here. I'm going to figure it out."

"If you do," she said, "would you call me? No, I mean it. Only after you get tickets, of course. I'll give you my number."

"Sure," I said. I took her name, Eve something, and her phone number, just to be polite. But I knew that as hard as I worked, as imaginative as I might be, and as lucky as I might get, there would never be an extra ticket to give to Eve. For the first time, I thought about the fact that there were other girls like Bridget and me out there. The difference between us was that we were going to get into the Beatles concert, somehow, some way, no matter what.

CHAPTER SEVEN

You Can't Do That

We were tired, but surprisingly, not terribly discouraged on our bus ride home from the Hollywood Bowl. It had been a long shot at best given our age, lack of ID, and our need to work on the one night that was going to be the Bowl's most challenging ever. A six-hour bus ride for each shift would have required serious patience, even from committed Beatles fans like us. There were other ways, we kept telling each other as we walked the last seven blocks home, although neither of us could yet provide specifics.

"You want to listen to the new record for a while?" I asked Bridget as we approached my house. The Beatles had released their second album only a few weeks earlier, and I had not yet listened to it the several thousand times I'd listened to the first one.

"Yeah. Let me go home and get something to eat first," she answered with a yawn. "See you in fifteen minutes maybe."

It was just as well it happened that way because of what I found in my bedroom. "Dad!" I exclaimed. He sat on the edge of one of my beds, leaning forward, elbows on his knees, listening intently to the Beatles singing "All My Loving." "What are you doing?"

"Hi, Annie." He smiled, and got up to lift the needle off the record. "I was just listening to some Beatles songs. I know how much you like them, and you know what? They're pretty darn good musicians."

My heart was beating faster than normal because this was just too weird. He didn't belong in the same room as the Beatles, much less listening to them. He belonged at his organ playing the worst songs ever written in the corniest ways ever heard. I was afraid that if he didn't leave, it might hurt the Beatles or something, infect them with a terrible musical virus.

"I'm working on some new songs for the Sunday shows," he said proudly. "I was thinking a Beatles medley might be really great. Bring in the kids. Show you that your old man is still hep!" And then he actually made a few moves that I think were supposed to be the Twist.

I thought I might faint. "Oh, Dad," I moaned, throwing myself into a chair. "You can't. It would—" I stopped before I said, "ruin them."

My smiling, loving, oblivious Dad then said, "I thought it would give us something to share. We both love music. This is new music for me. And it would give you a chance to appreciate what the Mighty Wurlitzer can do."

I closed my eyes, picturing him at the Mighty Wurlitzer at his Sunday concerts. It had at least four keyboards, about a thousand knobs you could pull to change the sounds, a shiny gold console that would have been perfect in a circus, and looked like it was made of frosting. Maybe there was a way to deter him, to lead him back to the road where songs like "Tea for Two" awaited him.

"Which of their songs did you like?" I tried to look pleasant, instead of like I wanted to throw up, which was closer to the way I felt.

"Well . . ." He picked up the record jacket to the Beatles first album. "'All I've Got to Do' has a great little rhythm thing going on. The organ was made for that." My mouth dropped open in horror. "And, let's see, it was on a 45 . . ." He glanced through a few records, turning them over to read the label on both sides. "Here it is. It's called 'This Boy.'"

"No," I whimpered.

"It's beautiful, really heartfelt. I was trying to find a third song for the medley when you came in."

"How about 'Till There Was You?'" The Beatles hadn't written it, so it wouldn't be ruined if he did one of his organ renditions of it.

He shrugged. "I'd rather do three Beatles tunes together. 'Love Me Do' had a kind of bluesy feel I could slow down—maybe put a little walking bass on it. What do you think?" I felt just like I would have if my Mother had asked me if she could make out with my boyfriend for a little while—totally violated.

This had to be nipped in the bud. "I have an idea, Dad. Why don't we try one of the songs now? That way, if it doesn't work out, you can go back to that other stuff you play."

He looked pleased. "I raised such a smart girl. Come on, let's go try." As I followed him to the living room, he said over his shoulder, "It's nice to have something to share with you again. It's hard to watch your child growing up and moving on. It's harder to find common ground."

I shook my head in disbelief as I trailed behind him. Why the Beatles? Why couldn't he just have stuck to his own awful music?

Slipping off his shoes so he wouldn't scuff the organ pedals, he seated himself on the smooth walnut bench. He pushed the on button, and I heard the familiar hum and waited for the weird speakers, the Leslies he called them, to start spinning. "They're what give the Hammond organ its extra special sound," he once told me.

They're what make me feel like I'm at a roller rink or a ballpark, I remember thinking.

He pulled some bars on the Hammond and adjusted a few knobs, and kind of sat up, hands on the keyboard feeling around for chords and melodies. My dad had an incredible ear. If you hummed a note, any note, he could tell you if it was a C or an E or an A or whatever. Within seconds I recognized "This Boy." I wanted to hate it so bad, but the beauty of the song made me actually appreciate what the organ did for it. It was weird for sure, but also beautiful, like seeing a favorite photograph covered by an inch of water. It moved differently, it was a little distorted, but fresh, too. Interesting.

Our front door opened. There stood Bridget with a horrified look on her face. She slowly walked over to where I was sitting and whispered, "Make him stop. Please make him stop." I glanced up at her. I swear her eyes were teary.

"Dad, look who's here!" I said loudly. He stopped playing and turned to look behind him.

"Hello, Bridget."

"Hi, Uncle Jim."

"Why are you playing a Beatles song?" she asked bluntly.

He smiled. "Do you like it?"

He began playing again. "I'm thinking of working up a little Beatles medley for the El Capitan shows."

Bridget's eyes narrowed, and she looked at me accusingly. I shook my head, and put a hand to my chest to indicate my innocence. "Sounds great," she said unenthusiastically, while motioning to me that she wanted to go to my bedroom and putting her hands over her ears and shaking her head for a second. "Come on, Annie. We have homework to do. Remember?" she said it like a robot or something.

"Oh, yeah. Sorry, Dad. Gotta go." I caught a glimpse of the disappointed look on his face as we hurried out of the room. I think he stopped playing.

When we got to my bedroom, Bridget closed the door firmly and then leaned against it as though we'd just escaped with our lives. "Annie. You've got to make him stop that. I mean it. It could ruin the Beatles for us!"

"I know. He's been listening to a bunch of their records. It's sick, it's horrible. That's our music, it's not for him."

"Yeah, he can have Doris Day, or . . . whoever he likes. Hands off the Beatles!"

"He's just trying to find a way to relate to me."

"He is related to you. He's your dad."

"I mean communicate."

Bridget lay down on my bed, staring at the Beatles pictures on the ceiling. "They communicate too much with us as it is. Why don't they leave us alone?"

"First our moms go back to school, and now my dad wants to play Beatles music. Maybe the end of the world really is getting nearer." I lay down on the other bed, my head at the foot. Ringo's face looked so strange upside down, all hair and nose. "What's our next plan?" I asked wearily. Bridget didn't answer. I sat up suddenly. "What about the Beatles fan clubs? Maybe they have a special 'in' to get tickets to the concert."

"Oh!" Bridget said, inhaling deeply and sitting up. "I can't believe we didn't think of that before! I'll bet they do. Where can we find one?"

"I don't know." My heart raced; this made sense. "Ah, ah . . . call the operator. See if one's listed."

She dove for the Princess phone and dialed O. "Hello, yes, I'm wondering if you have a listing for the Beatles fan club?" Her eyes got wide and she whispered, "Write this down, write this down: 429-7210. Would you repeat that please so I'm sure I got it right?" She said the number out loud again as I scribbled it in a notebook. Then she put the phone back in its cradle and looked at me proudly.

"This could be it," I said, amazed that we had a number in our hands that might be our "ticket" to the Beatles.

"This could be it," she repeated softly, and picked up the receiver again. "I'm going to call them right now. We don't have a minute to lose."

CHAPTER EIGHT

I'll Get You

The entire female student body of St. Boniface was in church Monday afternoon to practice for the May Day celebration. Not the fun one with the Maypoles and ribbons, or the serious one where the workers of the world show their unity. Our May Day celebration was to honor Mary, the Mother of Jesus, because May was dedicated to her. The boys of St. Boniface would arrive for practice only after the church had been emptied of girls.

"Why does she need an entire month all to herself?" Bridget whispered as we filed into one of the narrow spaces between the oak pews. We were on the far end of the side aisle, about six rows from the front.

"When you're God's mom, you get to throw your weight around, I guess." I heard the metal snap of a clicker, the favored instrument of our dean, Sister John of the Cross, known to all as John Boss. "Oh, God, here comes the unibrow."

She moved fast for a woman who could easily stand to shed forty pounds, and with a determined stride, the oversize rosary at her waist rattling like a muffler. She turned quickly, gracefully as she reached the altar rail and surveyed us—150 gently chattering girls in plaid skirts, boxy blue sweaters, and shapeless white shirts.

Click, click. She raised the device in the air, and the large arched ceiling of the church amplified the sound for her. I think if she could have gotten away with it, she would have used a whip. There was a general shuffling to attention, heads turning to the front of the church, some sat up straight, and all of us at least pretended she had our attention.

"Good afternoon, ladies." Her heavy features softened slightly to simulate a smile.

"Good afternoon, Sister," we answered as one. I felt grateful to be on the far aisle, away from her omniscient eye, free of the tension I would have felt if I'd been nearer to her.

"We're here today to perfect our devotion, our celebration, of the Virgin Mary."

"Virgin. I don't think so," Bridget whispered. I stifled a laugh.

"I know your homeroom teachers have gone over the program with you, including the prayers and the songs. We are going to go through it now. It will take about an hour. There will be no bathroom breaks, no running to the water fountain." Moans and protestations were just below the threshold of sound, but John Boss heard them all.

"And one more thing. Anyone speaking, laughing, not paying attention, or misbehaving in any way will be sent to stand in the back of the church until we are done. And you will be there again on Saturday from eight to two helping decorate the church and the statues. Have I made myself clear?"

"Yes, Sister."

"She's such a witch," I whispered without moving my lips.

"Don't talk," Bridget answered, looking straight ahead, her lips as immobile as mine had been. "Saturday is the Beatles fan club meeting. We can't miss it."

"Open your programs to page two, please. The organ will be playing during the procession. Once seated, we'll open with the song, 'Bring Flowers of the Rarest.'" She pulled a round thing the size of a yo-yo out of one of her pockets, and blew on it. It gave us our starting note. "Ready? Begin." John Boss swung her arms like a conductor.

"Bring flowers of the rarest, bring flowers of the fairest," we sang, through four dirgelike, a cappella verses.

Click, click. "Be seated. Look at your programs, please. You see that the invocation prayers are next, and then it says simply, 'song.' That song is one you're all familiar with, one you all love—" And then she actually paused to smile." 'Dominique'!"

Murmured sounds of pleasure swept through the church. Some girls even began to sing it softly. It was an OK song, I guess, but a nun singing for entertainment purposes had kind of ruined it for me.

"Students from the boys school will be joining us with their guitars to accompany us. Someone open the side door on my left, please." The side door on the opposite side of the church was opened, and the boys dean, Father Dismas, well known for his right hook, came in with three boys, each carrying a guitar and a folding chair.

"Oh, look," Bridget whispered, "it's Fondly. I didn't know he played the guitar." Fondly was the nickname we'd given to the short but very sweet Brad Huxley. It was the word he chose to sign above his name on the five or six cards he'd sent to Bridget last year, though he never did get up the nerve to ask her out.

"I think he might have grown a little," she said softly. Brad was a full six inches shorter than Bridget, which bothered her because being tall bothered her. "Imagine if Cynthia Lennon was six inches taller than John," she said one day. "It would be freakish."

"Freakish," I concurred. "Beatle wives must definitely be shorter than Beatle husbands."

"Silence!" John Boss thundered as the girls talked among themselves. "I don't want to hear one word until the lyric sheets have been passed out, and we're ready to sing." We stared at her mutely. "Colleen Cameron, I want you to give me whatever's in your hand." The poor girl stood uncertainly. "But, Sister, it's just a clip I was putting back in my hair because it fell out and . . ."

"Now. I want it now. And I want you to go to the back of the church and remain there until the end of our practice."

"That's so unfair," I whispered. John Boss with her batlike hearing turned her head our way. I made my face blank and immobile.

"Anyone else want to join her? Don't forget, it means you're here on Saturday, too." It was so quiet I could almost hear the tear roll down Colleen Cameron's cheek. John Boss turned back to her conversation with Father Dismas. The boys set up their chairs at the front of the church, and quietly tuned their instruments.

Several girls were passing out lyric sheets, and they eventually made their way down the row to us. I felt the nudge of Bridget's elbow against my arm. She'd taken a tiny spiral notebook and pen out of her purse; she passed them to me. Her note, referring to St. Dominic, who the song was written about, read, "Isn't Dominic the one that invented the rosary?"

"Ewww!" I responded. "Plus the Dominicans ran the Inquisition. I think."

Singing "Dominique" in French was one thing, all cute and Frenchie, and you think you're making Frenchlike sounds really good, and impressing yourself. We were handed the English translation to sing. Do you know what it actually says when you take all the French out? That Dominic was some poor idiot homeless guy who traveled around, and the one and *only* thing he talked about was "The Lord."

"This is going to be a pukefest," Bridget wrote.

"Focus on Fondly. See if you can tell how tall he is."

John Boss surveyed her captive girls. "Margaret Peterson, please come to the front."

"Such a suck-up!" Bridget scribbled. Margaret Peterson was the president of Sodality, our Catholic fan club for Mary. From what I heard, they pretty much sat around at their meetings and talked about how bitchin' Mary was. Margaret's thin, straight blond hair fell to her shoulders and never moved. I think that's because she had a habit of never moving her head from side to side, just her eyes. If she had to turn, her whole body went, like she had an invisible brace on or something. Freakish, as Bridget would say.

"Miss Peterson will sing the English lyrics for you once," John Boss announced. "The second time you will sing along with her."

The musicians began strumming, and after a few bars, Margaret joined in. It wasn't that she was so bad; it was just that the song was so bad in English. It was as though someone decided to put the text of a physics book to the tune of "Dominique." "If two electrons with the same polarization try to go to the same point in space and time, the interference is always negative." You get the idea. Margaret's eyes slid from side to side when she finished.

"I'll bet she doesn't even have a favorite Beatle," I wrote to Bridget, as we waited for our turn to join her in this spellbinding musical tour de force.

"Dave Clark Five girl for sure."

"Please stand," John Boss said, "and sing with Miss Peterson. I'd like you to go through it three times." The dreadful thing began again. We sang along with the motionless Margaret, but I was also checking out one of the guitarists. I'd seen him a few times, and he had a different kind of name. Royce, maybe? We started our second round of the same stupid verse, when out of the corner of my eye to the left, I caught a glimpse of black. John Boss was sneaking up on somebody. Bridget turned just in time to see her grab the notebook off the pew where we'd been sitting.

"That's mine," Bridget said, reaching for it.

"Not anymore." She walked away as the girls kept singing, reading the notes we'd written.

"We're dead," I whispered, barely breathing.

"I hate her," Bridget answered.

John Boss walked slowly toward us, put her face so close to ours I could see the hair on her face and said, "Pukefest? Get out, both of you, right now."

The girls around us were trying to see and hear as much as possible without getting into trouble themselves. "Go to the back and stay there until the church is empty. I don't want to see either of you sitting down. You'll be here Saturday at 8 a.m."

"No, Sister, we can't," I said. John Boss stopped moving.

"Excuse me?"

"We can't come on Saturday. We have a prior commitment."

She opened her mouth as if she was both shocked and almost amused by such cheek. "One more word and you're here every Saturday this month."

We walked to the back of the church, and stood across the aisle from the forlorn Colleen Cameron. I looked at the people who filled the church in front of me: the girls, the nuns, the priest, and I hated every one of them. I hated Mary for her greedy takeover of May, and this stupid ceremony, and John Boss most of all. Why were the teachers so hateful? Why was every activity aimed at killing any bit of life and fun you had in you?

I'd show up on Saturday because I had to or be kicked out of school, but I was going to leave in time for the Beatles fan club meeting. To test the correctness of my position, I spoke directly to the Almighty. "OK, God. If you don't want me to go to the Beatles meeting on Saturday, let the walls of this church come tumbling down." I waited a full thirty seconds. Nothing happened. It was all the proof I needed. If God Himself wasn't going to stand in my way, I'd find out how to step right over John Boss, and never look back.

CHAPTER NINE

Boys

Two hours later, free from John Boss and St. Boniface, we made our way to Zucky's delicatessen, where lots of kids hung out after school. We rolled up our skirts as we walked until they were a comfortable three inches above our knees. Zucky's smelled like kosher pickles, warm bagels, and pastrami. You could buy a bagel for fifteen cents at the counter, and sneak it over to the table and eat it, where they charged you fifty cents for the same thing if you ordered it off the menu. The waitresses got mad if they caught you, and wouldn't refill your coffee.

Bridget and I took a number and stood in front of the deli counter and discussed what to do. "I've had enough of getting caught for one day," I said, just as a girl in a St. Boniface uniform came to stand next to us.

"Hey," she said, with a quick glance at the two of us.

"Hi, Tina." She was one of the girls from Venice, a town about five miles south of Santa Monica. The Venice girls were generally poor, tough, and they stuck together.

"I like your hair," Bridget said. Tina's thick, dark hair was short in the back, teased up high in the front, and had curls that looped behind her ears.

"Thanks," she said matter-of-factly. "John Boss gave you a hard time, huh?" A note of admiration crept into her voice.

"Screw her," Bridget said.

"She thinks we're going to be there on Saturday," I said, trying to adopt a little tough-girl attitude of my own. "Yeah—as if."

"You're gonna bail on her?"

"Well . . . for part of it," I said, my rebel pose fading quickly.

"Part?" She turned to the counterman who looked at us impatiently. "Gimme four of those." She pointed to some square cookies. "So, you said *part*?"

"Yeah, there's somewhere we've gotta be. We're trying to get some tickets to a Beatles concert that's sold out already." I didn't want to mention it was a fan club meeting and look like a dork.

She shrugged. "You should just sneak in. That's what we do." Now she had our complete attention. We turned and stood directly in front of her, and moved in several inches closer.

"Where? How?" I asked.

"In El Monte, at the Legion Stadium. It's not that hard."

"How do you get in?" Bridget was completely focused on the answer.

"Different ways. Usually one girl and her boyfriend pay to get in, and then they unlock the bathroom windows and we all get in that way."

"Too cool," I said, wondering how we could apply this information to the Hollywood Bowl.

"When we go to the drive-in, we got three in the trunk, but only pay for the two they can see in the front seat."

"God, you know so much!" Bridget said admiringly. "Who drives?"

"My boyfriend."

"Wow."

"Do you like the Beatles?" I asked.

She shrugged a little. "They're OK."

"OK!" we replied in unison. She handed her money to the counter man, who gave her a small white bag.

"I'm more into the East L.A. scene. Thee Midniters, the Gallahads, Little Julien Herrera, you know."

"Yeah," I said nodding, not knowing what she was talking about.

"They're like the Beatles of East L.A. And those tickets are never sold out. They just keep stuffing people into the building. See ya," she said, and she turned and walked away.

I watched her in awe. Not only was her skirt rolled so it hit the middle of her thigh, she had a boyfriend with a car *and* she knew how to sneak into the El Monte Legion Stadium. It was beyond impressive.

"This opens up whole new worlds," I said to Bridget. "Let's go sit down." After a short wait, we slid across the bench seats of a wide booth next to the windows that lined the entire side of the building.

We ordered, and just as the waitress set down two cups of coffee, I said, "Bridget. Don't turn around. It's Fondly and that other guy. I think they're coming in."

She grabbed the rim of her thick coffee cup as if to steady it, managing to spill a fair amount into the saucer and burn her fingertips in the process. I handed her my napkin. "Are you nervous about seeing him?"

"Not exactly. I mean, I like him and everything, but he never asked me out. Remember?"

"Of course I remember. We only talked about it a thousand times."

"Should we ask them to sit with us?"

"I don't know. Do you think they would?"

"Guys are weird. Maybe." Her eyes narrowed as she watched them come in the front door and wait to be seated.

My back was to them. "Are they coming this way?"

"Yes," she said breathlessly. We pretended to be calmly drinking our coffee as the hostess led them by us on the way to their table.

"Oh, hey," Bridget said, as if surprised to see them. Fondly was in the lead.

"Hi," he said bashfully, slowing down just enough that Royce ran into him.

"Do you know my friend Annie?" She motioned toward me as if he wouldn't know who she was talking about otherwise.

"No, hi." He lifted his arm at the elbow to give me something between a wave and a salute. "Oh, ah, do you know Royce?"

We shook our heads. "This is Bridget and, uh . . ."

"Annie." I smiled and looked at Royce who seemed far more relaxed than Fondly.

"Do you boys still want this table?" the hostess called from a good ten feet away.

"I'll grab it," Royce said, leaving Fondly behind to stare at Bridget.

"You guys played really good today," I said, referring to their accompaniment of the dreadful "Dominique."

"Thanks. Yeah, it was weird, huh? In English and everything."

Bridget noticed something on his hands. "Did you do that playing guitar?" I saw abrasions on the knuckles of his left hand.

"Oh, no. Me and my friend, we snuck into Greystone and I scraped it on the way out."

"What's Greystone?" I asked as Bridget continued her visual inspection.

"Oh, it's so cool." He moved as he spoke, a little like a marionette on a loose string. "It's like a mansion on acres of land. Right in Beverly Hills. The Dohenys used to live there," he said, referring to an old, prominent family who had a major street named after them.

"Why did you have to sneak in?"

"Oh, nobody lives there. Not for a long time. It's dark, there aren't any lights. It's a cool place to go."

"Gosh, I'd love to see it!" Bridget smiled at him, and our dear, shy Fondly finally found the nerve to do what I know he'd been wanting to do for at least a year.

He motioned with his thumb back toward Royce. "Me and Royce were thinking of going Friday night. Do you think you . . ." He looked at Bridget, then at me, and back at her again.

"Yeah," Bridget said. "That sounds like fun." Then he sort of pointed at me.

"Both of us? That would be good. Do you want to check with your friend first, or . . ."

"Oh, no. He's cool. So, this is great." For one shining moment he stood still, looked Bridget right in the eye, and smiled.

"We live next door to each other, so that's easy," Bridget said with a nervous laugh. "What time?"

"Uh . . . seven?"

"Do you want my address?"

"Sure."

"It's 619 Marguerita. I don't have a pen or paper or anything." She looked at me meaningfully, remembering John Boss walking away with them, I'm sure.

"Can you remember?"

"619 Marguerita. Not a problem." He was weaving again.

"I think the waitress is waiting for you," I said, as Royce made a motion with his hand to get my attention.

"Yeah, better go. So . . . Friday." He turned, and barely missed knocking a tray full of water glasses out of the hands of an unsuspecting busboy.

Bridget looked at me wide-eyed and opened her mouth in a silent scream. "He finally did it!"

"It sounds kinda fun, too. A mansion, the dark, nobody home—"

Bridget made a little sound of delight. "I'll just wear flats. It doesn't matter if I'm still taller. Does it?"

"Will you get over the tall thing, please? All the models are tall."

"Except I don't look like them."

"I'll be there with a boy I don't even know!"

"He's pretty cute," she said with a smile.

"Listen," I said as our waitress delivered our overtoasted bagel, "I've got an idea. Tina said she and her friends sneak into their concerts, and Brad said he and his buddies sneak into Greystone. Put the two together. I'll bet you anything the guys could show us how to sneak into the Hollywood Bowl."

Bridget choked on her sip of coffee. "You are so right! Oh, my God. But remember how big it was? All those millions of seats?"

I paused, lowering my voice as if someone might be listening. "Do you remember what was at the very top of the last row?"

"Not really; it was all green and stuff."

"Exactly. It was ivy-covered ground. All we have to do is find the last street up there on the hill—"

"But there's probably a fence."

"Of course there's a fence, but we climb it, and whatever else they put in the way until we find that ivy."

"And then?"

"Either we sit in the ivy and listen, or sneak down to the seats."

"What if they catch us?"

"We'll run. Let them chase us. How are they going to find us among eighteen thousand other screaming girls?"

Bridget closed her eyes and exhaled deeply. "I think this could be the answer we've been waiting for."

I leaned to the left to peak around her to catch a glimpse of Brad and Royce. "We'll ask them about it on Friday at Greystone."

"It's perfect. My dad always says guys like a challenge."

"Then this should separate the men from the boys."

CHAPTER TEN

Don't Bother Me

We walked home from Zucky's excited and happy, but there were still two hurdles that lay ahead of us. Standing on the sidewalk in front of my house, we watched our mothers through the kitchen window as they talked and laughed.

"They look like they're in a good mood," Bridget said. "Let's ask them now, before our dads get home." I nodded my agreement.

"We need clearance on the Friday-night date," I began, "and a note to John Boss saying we have to leave early on Saturday."

"What time?"

"Eleven thirty. The meeting's in Westwood at noon. That should give us plenty of time."

"OK." Bridget squared her shoulders.

"Just remember, talk about the date first, John Boss second." We strolled into the kitchen with smiles on our faces.

"Hi, girls," my mom said, standing at the counter. Felicia stood next to her; several sheets of paper were spread out in front of them.

"What are you doing?" I asked.

The sisters glanced excitedly at each other. "We're planning our class schedule for UCLA." You know how people say somebody "glowed" with excitement? I actually saw that in my mom.

"It's so great," Bridget said, setting her books down on the kitchen table. "I'm really proud of you both."

"You are?" Her mom said it in a way that showed she wanted her daughter's approval.

"Of course," I responded. "How neat that you guys want to improve yourselves."

"And finish something we started," my mom added.

"You're great role models for us and stuff."

"I've never heard you say anything like that, Annie," my mother said, looking like it really touched her.

"If we ever graduate from St. Boniface, maybe we'll go there too."

"I'm sure it seems very far away, but it's just two more years. When you reach our age, you'll see that's a very short time."

"We had something new happen to us today at school," I said, trying to look excited and demure at the same time.

"What?" my mom asked as she filled a glass of water from the tap.

"Two boys asked Bridget and me on a double date on Friday." The sisters' mouths dropped open in exactly the same way.

"That's great," they said as one. Bridget and I hadn't exactly been on a lot of dates, and sometimes I think my mom worried about it.

"Tell us about them!" my Aunt Felicia said, pulling up a chair to the kitchen table to be near Bridget.

"We don't really know them that well," Bridget answered. "One is named Brad, he's my date, and he's a sophomore. And the other is Royce, and I think he may be a junior. Is he, Annie?"

"I'm not sure. I guess I'll find out on Friday night."

"Where are they taking you?" my mom asked.

Bridget and I exchanged a brief glance, having forgotten to create that part of the story. "We're going to go for ice cream," I said quickly. "And a movie." That would give us a pretty big hunk of time to go to Greystone, and hopefully to the Hollywood Bowl for a stakeout mission.

"How exciting," Bridget's mom said. "Do you know what you're going to wear?"

"Well," Bridget began, "I was more wondering what time we'd have to be home."

The sisters looked at each other; my mom took this one. "We'll discuss it with your fathers, but I'm guessing ten o'clock."

"Oh, Mom, see if you can talk them into 10:30. Because just think about it. They won't pick us up till seven, and then we have to drive to Westwood to the movie theater—"

"Yeah, all the way to Westwood," Bridget chimed in.

"—then park, then two hours at the movie, then walk to Wil Wright's for ice cream, then home. I mean, if you add that all up, we really should say eleven."

"I don't know, Annie. That's awfully late."

"Please Mom. Try, OK? That's all I ask." She smiled the way moms do when they're picturing you when you were a baby.

She nodded. "We'll see what we can do."

"And there's one more thing," I said, "before you get back to making your schedules 'cause I know how important that is." I cringed hearing myself sound like such a kiss-up, but this could get tricky. "The dean wants us to help decorate the church on Saturday morning for the May procession on Sunday."

"How nice."

"From like eight in the morning till two in the afternoon."

Aunt Felicia's eyebrows went up. "That's a long time."

"Exactly, that's just the point I was getting to. Bridget and I have received an invitation to join a Beatles fan club," I said, embellishing the truth a little, "and our first meeting is Saturday at noon."

The sisters eyed each other as if sharing secret, special memories. "Frank Sinatra!" I exclaimed. "You used to go see him, right? So you guys know just how we feel."

"And how important it is," Bridget added.

Aunt Felicia laughed and sighed. "Oh, could he sing!"

"I don't see why you couldn't leave a little early to go to the meeting," my mom added, putting a few dishes in the cupboard.

"The thing is, we'll need a note." Maybe it was my delivery, or maybe it was their mom radar, but the expressions on both of their faces changed slightly.

"Why would you need a note when you're volunteering your time on a Saturday?"

"It's not *exactly* voluntary."

They stood silent, waiting for an explanation.

"The dean *hates us*!" Bridget said suddenly. "She's just as mean as she could be. One girl has to come on Saturday because a barrette fell out of her hair and she was just trying to put it back in."

"That makes no sense," my mom said.

"Exactly!" Bridget exclaimed. "And all we did was write one note to each other so we wouldn't disturb the other girls, and now she wants to ruin our Saturday and our chance to see the Beatles."

Her Mom folded her arms over her chest. "What you're trying to say is you were caught passing notes, and you're being punished by having to help on a Saturday."

"No! That's not it, because the dean is so unreasonable she'll grab at anything just to make you feel bad."

"But you were passing notes?" my mom asked me.

"Yes."

"And you got caught?"

"Yes."

"Then this is your punishment for breaking the rules." She turned away, and ran the water to do some dishes.

"You don't understand," Bridget pleaded. "We have to be at the Beatles meeting. Otherwise we may never get a chance to go to their concert."

"I'm sorry," her mom said, joining her twin at the sink. "That's how you learn self-control, and personal responsibility."

I felt like I would explode with frustration. "And what if you're at UCLA and you get sick and miss a test—is this how you want the professor to treat you?"

"That's different," my mom answered. "That's an illness, not an act of free will."

"But Mom, you put us there! You make us go to a school where they treat us like we're the enemy."

Bridget stood up to make the point more effectively. "And if you learn something, it's in spite of them taking all the interesting stuff out of it."

"You girls," her mom scoffed. "You'd think you were at a prison."

"But it is!" I said. "No one listens to us, no one cares what we think or want or need. And we get punished for everything. I feel like Jane Eyre!"

"Annie, really, you have a flair for the dramatic. The answer is still no. If you passed notes, this is your punishment."

"We'd be doing you a disservice if we did anything else," Felicia added.

Bridget grabbed her books. "Let's go to my house, Annie," she said icily.

I was so mad, I wanted to cry. "I hope you think about the Golden Rule all day Saturday," I said as we were leaving. "We would never try to keep you from something you loved. Imagine if we said you were bad moms for going back to school!"

"We're not bad moms for going back to school," my aunt said, sounding defensive.

"You won't be here as much. Your attention will be elsewhere. We're teenage girls who need guidance and leadership. But never in a million years, would I try to keep you from what you loved!" I headed for the back door so they wouldn't see I had tears in my eyes.

"Not in a million years!" Bridget repeated dramatically, and followed me out the door.

A few minutes later, we were lying on the beds in Bridget's room, listening to George Harrison sing "Don't Bother Me" like he really meant it.

"What are we going to do now?" Bridget asked, staring up at the picture of Paul on the ceiling.

"I'm going to write a note and pretend my mom wrote it. I'm pretty good at forging her signature."

"What if John Boss finds out? We'd get in so much trouble."

"I know. Are you willing to miss the Beatles meeting?"

"No," she admitted.

"Me neither. Maybe John Boss will figure it out, maybe not."

"What if she calls your mom right then and asks?"

"There's no phone in the church. If she goes somewhere to call her, we'll leave."

"Yeah, maybe forever."

"They still wouldn't understand."

"No, they wouldn't."

We joined George in singing "Don't Bother Me," and we really meant it, too.

CHAPTER ELEVEN

There's a Place

After much begging and pleading, our parents decided we could be home from our date by 10:45. They postponed dinner and waited with us on Friday night in Bridget's living room as if this was the biggest thing that had ever happened to us.

"Do you think you could take off your Tam o' Shanter, Dad?" Bridget asked.

"Take off me bonnet? Absolutely not!" The grown-ups found this amusing; I was just relieved he hadn't added a kilt and knee socks.

"I think we're going to, you know, wait outside for them," I said, walking backward toward the front door. Bridget had her purse over her shoulder and was practically running toward me before I'd finished my sentence.

"Oh, no," my mom said. "You'll wait right here young lady. A man won't respect a girl he doesn't have to treat well."

"We're just trying to make it more convenient for them, Aunt Joyce," Bridget explained.

"Men don't like convenience," her father interjected. "They like the hunt."

"What are we—bison?" I asked, frustrated, wanting them all to be safely locked up in their rooms with their straitjackets on, away from us and our business. The doorbell rang.

"I'll get it," I practically shouted before any of them could move. A certain thrill shot through me when I opened the door and saw Brad and Royce standing there, looking clean, handsome, and a little nervous.

"Hi. Come on in." All four of our parents stood up, to get a better look at them.

I made introductions. The boys gave the fathers manly handshakes, and a nod and a "Pleased to meet you, ma'am," to our mothers.

All six of us then stood in awkward silence until my father broke it. "I understand you boys are musicians."

"A little," said Brad.

"We play some guitar, sir," Royce offered.

"You know, I'm a musician myself. I've got a beauty of an organ next door if you'd like to see it." I thought I would drop dead of embarrassment.

"Uh, Dad, we have a movie to see and everything."

Bridget moved quickly toward the front door. "Maybe next time, Uncle Jim. We'll tell them about how good you are." I knew Bridget would have thrown herself across the keyboard to keep him from playing.

"Now don't keep these lassies out too late," Uncle Thomas said.

I could tell the boys caught his strange accent, and so to avoid inquiries or further conversation I said, "OK, then, bye-bye."

"We'd like you to have the girls back by 10:45," my dad said.

"Yes, sir," Brad answered. "We'll definitely have them home by then."

"Ten forty-five," Royce repeated. And with little waves and murmured good-byes, we were out the door. I felt about a hundred pounds lighter.

Royce was driving an aqua blue Dodge, confirming my belief that he was sixteen. I sat up front with him, but near the door. Everyone knows you don't sit right next to a boy until the third date. Glancing over my shoulder, I noticed Brad was not only sitting next to Bridget but had his arm up over the seat and rested his hand on her shoulder. I guess it was a little different for them because he'd sent her all those "Fondly" cards; it kind of speeded up the process.

"You told your dad we're going to a movie?" Royce glanced over at me.

"We had to tell them something."

Bridget laughed. "We couldn't exactly say we were going to break into an old mansion in the dark!"

"Where's your dad from?" Bridget hesitated.

"Madison," I answered for her.

"Wisconsin?"

"No, Ireland. Madison, Ireland. But he's been here since he was a baby. The accent, it kind of lingers."

"He owns The Shamrock, the Irish and Scottish shop downtown," Bridget said. "Sometimes he gets confused and thinks he's Scottish. But then he'll talk about St. Patrick like he actually knew him or something. It's weird."

"What else did you tell your dad we were going to do?" Royce asked me. I decided to ignore a certain suggestiveness in his voice.

"Go to Wil Wright's for ice cream."

"Hey, that's a good idea," Brad said. "First Greystone, then Wil Wright's. Most excellent."

"My grandma gave me a gift certificate for my birthday last year to Wil Wright's. It took me all summer to use up twenty dollars!" Bridget said.

"When's your birthday?" Brad wanted to know.

"June 18th. It's also—"

"Paul McCartney's birthday," Brad broke in excitedly.

Bridget practically screamed. "How did you know that!?"

"I'm a righteous Beatles fan. Don't you like them?"

"Like them?" we said in unison.

"I *love* them," Bridget said.

"All we can think about is how we can get to see them at the Bowl this summer," I added.

"Do you have tickets?" Royce asked, obviously misunderstanding what I'd said.

"No, I meant we're trying to figure out ways to get them."

"They're sold out," Royce said, as if this was a news flash.

"That's what I hear." I didn't want to go into any of our plans, explanations, or dreams about getting to see the Beatles.

"Do either of you guys have tickets?" Bridget asked.

"No," Brad answered, "wish I did. I'd take you if I did." I looked over my shoulder. Bridget looked at him like he'd just grown six inches.

"Would you really?"

"You bet." He moved a little closer to her, and she let him.

I glanced out of the corner of my eye at Royce. He was a cooler type than Brad, maybe more introspective. Even though we were on a date, I couldn't tell yet if he even liked me.

Royce made his way quickly over to Sunset Boulevard. There were faster ways to get to Beverly Hills, but this was the prettiest, winding through the westside hills. We drove past the west gate of Bel Air just before we came to Dead Man's Curve, the place the song was written about. It doesn't seem that bad until you're in it, picking up speed as you race downhill. Then suddenly, WHAM, you're trying to turn left at a right angle. That's where all the crashes are. It's hairy.

The winding road straightens out just as you hit Beverly Hills. From there, it was just a mile or so till we made the left turn that took us onto Foothill Drive, and to Greystone Mansion. We parked across the street from the entrance. I could see a wide driveway blocked off by a ten-foot-high wrought-iron gate, with a large stone gatehouse on the left, and a ten-foot stone wall on each side of it that looked like it surrounded the property.

"How do we get in?" I asked, hoping I wasn't expected to squeeze between the bars.

"You climb that tree," Royce said pointing to the right, "and then you get on top of that flat stone wall. You just climb down the wall from there."

"Just climb down?" Bridget repeated doubtfully.

"It slopes out, and it's uneven," Brad assured her. "It's sort of like steps, only different."

"OK," I said, opening the car door, "let's try it." I tucked my purse under the passenger seat so I could have both hands free in case I fell to my death.

The air was luscious, filled with the fragrance of the Victorian Box trees that grew in hedges along the street. It was just past twilight, but there were no streetlights, and so it seemed darker. Bridget and I peered through the gate. A wide driveway broke quickly off to the left, and then eased back to the right on its way to the big house.

"Wow," I said, catching only the silhouette of the great mansion against the sky. It was enormous, seeming to stretch for a good two blocks from side to side.

Brad came up next to Bridget and put his arm around her waist. "How many times have you done this?" I asked, feeling nervous, excited, and a little scared.

"Like four times," Brad said.

"And you?" I asked Royce.

"This will be my second time."

"I'll show you," Brad said, moving toward the tree. "It's easy." He pulled himself up quickly into the medium-size tree next to the wall on the right.

"You just stretch yourself over and get on top of the wall." Just as he was about to haul himself from the tree to the wall, we heard a voice coming from behind the gate, not six feet from where we stood.

"May I help you?" A flashlight shined in our eyes, almost blinding us. Bridget and I made little sounds of being startled and afraid.

"Ah, no sir," Royce said nervously, glancing quickly up at Brad in the tree. The man's flashlight followed Royce's gaze and shined brightly on Brad, who was trying to crouch behind one of the bigger branches of the tree.

"OK, son. I want you to get down from there." As Brad jumped down, the light swung back on us.

"Now listen to me," the voice behind the light said. "This is private property. I don't want to see you kids around here anymore. You understand me?"

"Yes, sir," we all said. I couldn't see the man, or if he was wearing a uniform, but it was clear we weren't going to enter the mansion grounds on his watch.

"Now go on. Get in your car before I take your license plate number down."

Without protest or conversation, we hustled back to the Dodge and got in. I locked my door; Bridget saw me do it and locked hers.

"That was close," Brad said. I thought I heard a tinge of embarrassment in his voice.

"That's never happened before?" I asked.

"Nope. I know lots of guys who've done it, too. There's never been anybody there."

Royce turned toward the three of us. "What do you want to do?"

This was my chance. "You guys seem good at sneaking into places—I mean, except for just now. Do you think you could help us find a way to sneak into the Hollywood Bowl?"

Royce put the car in Drive. "Let's go."

"We'll figure it out," Brad said happily. "When we do, maybe we could all four go to see the Beatles together."

"Great." As long as Bridget was with me I didn't care who I went with.

We settled in for the short drive to the Bowl. It was still early. There was plenty of time to be home by 10:45.

CHAPTER TWELVE

I'll Cry Instead

Royce seemed most comfortable asking questions. "What's your favorite class?" English. "What's your favorite song?" "She Loves You." "What's your favorite TV show?" Maybe *Jack Paar* or *Candid Camera.* The conversation didn't go anywhere after I asked him the same questions back. Although it was kind of revealing when he said his favorite singer was Dick Dale, because Dick Dale never sings when he plays his weird, wonderful surf guitar thing. It meant that either Royce had a vivid imagination, or he was totally full of it.

We turned onto the last street before you entered the Hollywood Bowl, and kind of followed our noses up the narrow streets. "I think you're going in the wrong direction," Brad said to Royce as the road switch-backed, and then turned again. He and Bridget had been so silent in the back seat, I thought maybe they were making out and that Royce's quiz questions just covered up the sound.

"I know," Royce answered, "but we're still climbing. I'm going to keep going until we come to a dead-end street. Chances are that will be the top of the Hollywood Bowl property."

"I was thinking the same thing," Brad said, but I don't think he was thinking about anything but Bridget, but guys seem to like to think they come up with everything first.

"The houses are so close together," I said, rolling down the window and peering into the darkness. "We need to find some with open yards on the side so we can get back in there and look around."

Royce nodded. "Can you read that street sign?"

I could barely make it out in the dark. "Los Tilos Road."

"I'm gonna turn here. See where the moon is? I think that's about where the Hollywood Bowl is, so I'm going to follow that." In less than a minute, we were in a cul-de-sac, with the moon in front of us. "I think this is it." Royce parked and killed the headlights. None of us spoke; it was quiet and dark.

As my eyes adjusted to the dim light, I said, "What's that over there?" and pointed forward and to the left. "I think it's a little hill, but it doesn't look like it belongs. I bet that's the back of it."

"I'm stoked, let's boogie," Brad said, opening the back door. The crickets were busy, and the air smelled of sage. I thanked God that reptiles tucked themselves in their warm beds at night, and I wouldn't have to worry about them.

Bridget and Brad held hands. I fought the urge to walk next to her, and followed Royce to the hill. There was a four-foot cyclone fence in front of it that took us only seconds to get over. The hill looked man-made, even in the dark, because it was smooth and uniform in shape and had only ragged clumps of weeds burrowing their way out of it.

The soft, gravely soil meant death and destruction for my new espadrilles, but going barefoot was not an option. A fifteen-foot hill looks pretty small until you start to climb it. By the time I got to the top, I was breathing hard.

When we crested the hill we stopped and stared down at the empty, ghostly Hollywood Bowl, lit only by the waning moon. The white stage and the half-dome band-shell covering it was easy to spot, but it looked impossibly far away. That's where the Beatles will be, I thought, right there. I wondered how close or how far away from the stage I'd be on that night.

"I can't believe it was this easy!" Bridget said in a low voice.

"We're not in yet." I gazed down at the forty yards of darkness that I guessed ended where the last of the bench seats were installed.

"It's like a sea of ivy," Brad observed, slipping his arm around Bridget. He was moving pretty fast for a guy who couldn't get past "Fondly" for an entire school year. "We can swim this baby, no problem. This is way easier than Greystone. I'm thinking I'll be seeing a lot of Bowl concerts this year." The guys laughed and seemed to think that was a great idea. I could only justify sneaking in for the Beatles. My almost physical need to see and hear them was overriding the ethical rules I'd had drilled into me. There's always confession, I assured myself, as I looked hard at the ivy patch to see if there was a best way to get down into it.

Once there, I took my first step forward. The ivy was thick and deep, which also made it uneven because we were stepping into layers and years' worth of growth. Royce was about ten feet to my left, Bridget on my right, and Brad next to her. If Brad hadn't been holding her hand, I would have held on to it, because it was a treacherous process walking downhill in the thick stuff, and I wasn't about to grab onto Royce. Twice I almost lost my balance as my foot slipped several inches into the lower growth of the ivy. My feet felt dirty, and were getting scratched. I felt like a bottomless pit was going to open up in front of me, and I would fall endlessly.

The pitch of the hill was steeper than it seemed at first, increasing a sense of imbalance and forward motion. If I could have been assured a soft landing, I might have tried to roll down.

"John and Paul!" Bridget called to me.

"George and Ringo," I answered. It helped. We weren't even halfway down yet, and I wanted to turn back. Moonlight was good for mood and for seeing big things like the stage, but it didn't really help you see that much better in the dark.

"How far down do you want to go?" Royce sounded less than enthusiastic.

"All the way!" Brad answered. My choice was made. I could put up with the yukiness of this part if it landed us in the Hollywood Bowl on August 23rd.

"It's not that bad," Bridget added, but I could hear the discomfort in her voice.

We'd passed the halfway mark. I could see a fence up ahead that I assumed surrounded the edge of the Bowl property, but I couldn't tell how tall it was. The farther downhill we went, the darker it got, because the ivy now engulfed us. I focused my mind on a mental picture of the Beatles and sang softly to myself, "All my loving . . ." In August, I reminded myself, the Bowl would be filled, there would be lights, we'd be familiar with this part—the whole experience would be much easier. I looked up, knowing I had the strength to do this tonight, and once more in August.

Then came the voice out of the darkness: harsh, male, robotic. "You are now trespassing on private property. Stop where you are. Security guards are on their way." We all stopped moving. As if to emphasize the point, sprinklers went on from the front, and sides, and even behind us. The voice repeated its message: "You are now trespassing on private property . . ."

"Oh, God," Bridget exclaimed.

I was torn. The uppermost part of the Bowl was close now; I would reach it in less than a minute if I didn't fall. I was already wet. It would take the security guys a few minutes to get to us. It might be my only chance to see what other surprises could greet us in August.

I turned to my left. Royce was walking back to the top of the hill, muttering something I couldn't understand. The hiss of the sprinklers was loud.

"Bridget! Should we go back?"

There was silence.

Finally I heard, "No! Let's go all the way."

"I don't think so," I heard Brad tell her uneasily. "Come on, let's turn around."

"You don't understand. I have to go. But you don't have to go with me."

I heard the sound of footsteps in the ivy, and knew it was Bridget pushing forward.

"I'm here, Bridget," I cried, moving toward her, able only to see an outline of my cousin. "Let's run. Grab my hand."

You couldn't call what we did next running exactly. It was more the way you run in the ocean, or the snow—lots of effort and exaggerated motion, not much progress. I started laughing at the ridiculous situation in which we'd put ourselves; Bridget joined in. The water was cold, we were both soaked, but the goal was near.

"We're almost to the fence!" Bridget cried.

"Ahhhh!" I yelled, moving forward as fast as I could.

"Do you think it's electrified?"

"I don't know, but we'll soon find out."

In another five seconds, we sort of ran right into it because we couldn't stop our forward momentum.

"We didn't get electrified!" Bridget shrieked, rolling against it. I clung to it with both hands, catching my breath, and trying to see what lay beyond it.

"We did it! I can't believe we made it," Bridget said, panting.

"I know, I know. Hey, look down there. What is that?" I squinted to make out what I thought was another fence about ten feet away.

"I can't quite see," Bridget responded, then walked to her right. "Here's a sign."

I followed. "Can you read it in the dark?"

"Yeah, I think. 'Danger'—as if we didn't know." She giggled. "'Do not climb fence. 30 foot drop to cement bottom.'"

"What?"

"Oh, my God. 'Could result in permanent injury or death.'"

I knelt down to see if I could see beyond the fence and make sense of what the sign said. I had to move twice, because a stream of water from a nearby sprinkler was hitting me in the face. Bridget did the same. It looked dark, but a different kind of dark than the ivy.

"Bridget!" I exclaimed. "It's like a moat, but empty and made of cement."

"No!"

"I can't even see the bottom."

"We could have fallen to our deaths!"

"Maybe. The fence is only about ten feet high. Of course we would have assumed there was ground on the other side."

"But we would have fallen and died!"

"Or just lay there until the Beatles played, and then died."

Bridget started to laugh, then stopped. "That's not funny."

I sat back on my heels, wet, cold, happy, and frustrated. "On the night of the concert, we could just sit in the ivy at the top, before where the sprinklers go on."

"That would work. I'm not climbing this fence, even for the Beatles."

"We could lay a ladder across from this fence to the next one, like a bridge," I said almost to myself, knowing that unless I grew wings between now and August, this was as close to the stage as I was getting if we came from this direction.

Bridget sighed and laughed a little as she said, "I wonder where the guys are?"

"In the car, dry, and waiting for us." We got to our feet.

"How are we going to explain our wet clothes to our parents?"

"We've got time to dry out," I told her, "but let's get out of here."

As we turned to start the long, wet, dark climb back up to the street, I heard voices raised in anger. "Bridget," I whispered, "what is that?"

"Maybe the security guys caught them! We need to get out of here now."

"Can you tell if it's Brad and Royce?"

"The sprinklers are too loud. Come on, let's hurry."

In five minutes we passed from the wet to the dry ivy, and in five more we were at the top of the little hill that bordered the street. We didn't hear the voices again.

"I would have thought they'd be here waiting for us," Bridget said with a touch of disappointment in her voice.

"Where's the car?" Getting down fifteen feet of dirt hill was easy compared to the ocean of ivy. "I must be turned around. I don't see it."

Bridget stood on the sidewalk, hands on her hips. "It's not here."

"What do you mean it's not here? It has to be." But I knew she was right. The little cul-de-sac was empty.

"Do you think that's what we heard?"

"What do you mean?" I asked.

"Those voices."

"Do you mean like they had an argument or something?"

"They had an argument all right." The gravely voice of an older man called out not fifteen feet to our left. We gasped in surprise.

"Who are you?" I cried, unable to see him.

A bald and bent man stepped out into the overhead light of his porch. "If you kids had any respect for the law, you wouldn't be up here."

"Where are they?"

"They left when I told them I was calling the police."

"They left?" Bridget repeated.

"What did they do, leave you two behind?"

"Yes, sir," I answered, as a feeling of panic began to build in my chest.

"Are they coming back?" Bridget asked, sounding forlorn.

"Not if they know what's good for them. I'm tired of you darn kids up here all the time."

"This is our first time," I explained. "Do you think we could use your phone to call our parents?"

The man looked up as if talking to the heavens, and praying for patience. "You most certainly may not." He turned, walked in the house, shut the door loudly, and turned off the porch light.

We stood there silently for a moment as our predicament sunk in.

"Did you bring any money with you?" Bridget asked.

"A dollar. How about you?"

"Maybe a dollar fifty."

"We can't even ride the bus home on that."

"I know. They wouldn't just leave us here . . . would they?"

"They already did."

"What are we going to do?" Bridget sounded like she might be panicking, too.

"First, let's comb our hair and put on lipstick, and try to look decent." It was harder than it sounded in the dark, and with wet cotton dresses clinging to us.

"At least we don't look like crazy people now," Bridget said, putting her brush back in her purse.

"Let's start walking down the hill. I remember the big streets the bus took when we came to the Bowl before. We can always walk if we have to."

Bridget almost choked. "Annie! That's fourteen miles. You told me that yourself."

"I know. Come on, maybe the guys are looking for us."

"Yeah. Probably they're waiting right around the corner." We hurried to the end of the street. We stood there for a minute, staring into the quiet, empty lane. No Brad, no Royce, no car. "Which way?"

"I'm guessing left, but I don't really know."

"Me neither, may as well try it." Ten minutes later, we were still wandering the labyrinthine streets of the Hollywood Hills. We went down, we went up again; we could have been going in circles for all we knew.

"I think I hear a car," I said. "Let's flag it down and see if they can tell us how to get out of here." It came around the corner slowly, its lights blinding us. I turned my head to the left to avoid looking into them, and waved with my right hand. The car squeaked to a halt five feet in front of us, its lights still blazing. I felt a little scared and vulnerable when I heard the passenger door open, and tried to stare past the harsh light.

"Need a ride, ladies?" It was Brad. I felt relief—and anger.

"I can't believe you just left us!" Bridget yelled, walking ahead of me, elbowing Brad out of the way, and getting into the passenger side of the front seat.

"We didn't really. This old guy came out and started yelling and—"

Bridget rolled up her window and stared straight ahead.

"Let's just go," I said to Brad, as I climbed in the back seat.

"But—" He stood outside the car for a moment, staring at Bridget. On the way home, he tried a few times to explain, but she wouldn't talk to him. I don't think either of them cared what I thought.

The only thing Royce said was, "Do you guys have a towel or anything you could sit on? My old man gets really hacked if I hurt his car."

"No we don't have any towels! Are you kidding?" I felt furious, even though it wasn't really his fault. I just wanted to be back in Santa Monica. "Drop us at 12th and Georgina," I said as we neared our neighborhood.

"Why?" Brad asked, and leaned forward as if Bridget would give him the answer.

"Because we can't go home like this. We've got to stop at our friend's house."

I admired Brad for his persistence, but when we got close to 12th street, with the car practically still moving, Bridget got out and marched straight for our friend Paula's house, calling out over her shoulder, "Thank you for a lovely evening."

"Bye, guys," I said, and followed Bridget to the back of the house, where we knocked on Paula's bedroom window.

She pulled the curtain back, and when she saw it was us, opened the window. "What happened to you guys?"

"We'll explain. Do you think we could dry our clothes here before we go home?"

"Sure. Meet me at the back door." For the next hour, we sat in two of Paula's bathrobes while our clothes spun in her dryer. When we told her what happened, it sounded funny already. Paula couldn't understand why Bridget was so mad at Brad.

"Because he didn't have it in him to keep going forward, and then he just left us there! Anything could have happened."

"You could have turned back when he did . . ."

Bridget looked horrified. "Did I not mention we're talking about the Beatles concert?"

"OK, it was kind of a cold thing for him to do. But nothing bad happened, and they came looking for you, right?"

"We're not sure," I said. "Maybe they couldn't find their way down either." For me it was a temporary setback; I was pretty sure I could come up with some more ideas about getting us into that concert. For Bridget, it was more. Brad had finally broken through from Fondly to contender, and now he was just somebody who disappointed her, and hurt her feelings.

When our clothes were dry and we'd made ourselves look presentable, we walked the five blocks to my house. On the sidewalk out front, we pretended we were saying goodnight to the boys for the sake of our parents, who we were pretty sure were listening. "Thank you, Royce. I had such a nice time," I called out into the darkness.

"Goodnight, Brad. Yeah, tomorrow. I'll talk to you then," Bridget said to the empty sidewalk.

We walked into my living room and there were our parents, sitting in a row on the couch, legs crossed in exactly the same way, with magazines on their laps as if they were reading. "Hi, girls," my mom said, all innocent. "Aren't you going to invite your dates in?"

"No, Aunt Joyce. They left already," Bridget said, and walked through the kitchen and out the back door to her house.

"We gave them a challenge, like you said," I told them.

"And?" my Uncle Thomas asked with a smile.

"They weren't up to it."

CHAPTER THIRTEEN

Devil in Her Heart

I was up at 5:30 composing the note from my mom to give to John Boss. "To Whom It May Concern." That gave it a kind of grown-up flourish, I thought, admiring how well I could imitate my mother's handwriting. "My daughter Annie Street and her cousin Bridget O'Malley must leave this morning no later than 11:30 a.m." I started to write something about a grandma dying, but that excuse was so overused; I decided to keep it vague. "They are required to be at a family gathering where they would be sorely missed if they were absent. Sincerely, Mrs. James Street." Girls don't use words like "sorely," so that made it more believable. I got some of my mom's stationery, the little cream-colored notes with the blue edge, and created the best forgery possible.

Bridget and I managed to keep our nervousness under control until just before we walked into the church at two minutes to eight. "I think John Boss can read minds," Bridget whispered.

"I'm pretty sure Satan has given her special powers, but this note is good. Besides, I'm willing to risk it. I am not missing that meeting today."

Bridget closed her eyes and murmured, "Beatles, Beatles, Beatles, Beatles. OK, I'm ready." We found out miracles were real when we took deep breaths, opened the heavy door, and found that dear, deaf, blind Sister Ignatius was in charge of decorating that morning.

"Good morning, Sister," I beamed, holding the note out for her. "I spoke with Sister John of the Cross already about this. Bridget O'Malley and I have to leave early today."

She squinted and held her ancient hand out for the note about two inches from where it was; I guided it in. She opened the envelope, and glanced at it for a second. "I'm sure that will be fine, dear."

"Should I tell you when it's time for us to leave?"

"Certainly."

"What time did my mom say? Was it eleven or eleven thirty?"

"I'm not sure, I . . ." She held it out to me so that I might read it to her.

"Oh, yes. Eleven."

She nodded.

"We'll come and say good-bye, Sister."

Knowing we'd be out by eleven made decorating the statues and the pews with flowers kind of fun. One enterprising boy who referred to himself as "the next Oleg Cassini" wove a three-foot banner of flowers and draped it diagonally across Mary's vaguely carved chest, making her look a little like a beauty contestant. But he was frustrated. "I want it to say 'Jackie,' but like in a holy way. And, excuse me, but is there ever going to be a statue of Mary where she's wearing shoes? Hullo! Earth to God—get your Mother some shoes, please!" By the time we left, he was making little slip-ons for her from red carnations.

"Thank you, Sister," we told Ignatius as we prepared to leave. She waved in our general direction and we were free. Running down the church steps toward the bus stop, we squealed and laughed from the success of our ruse, and the half hour we'd shaved off of our sentence.

Thirty minutes later we jumped off the bus in Westwood, and walked three blocks north of Wilshire until we came to the home of Patty Ewald, president of Beatles fan club No. 182. Her house was about twice the size of Bridget's house and my house put together. The front door was open, and we walked into a two-story entry hall. To the right was a wide arch that led into the living room.

A girl with oversize glasses greeted us. "Hi! Are you here for the meeting?" She was friendly and enthusiastic, and she waved at us to follow her into the huge oblong living room.

"Do you want us to sign in or anything?" I asked, a little nervous about the new setting, new people, and the richness of my surroundings.

"We are so excited!" Bridget lifted her shoulders, and then sort of dropped them back down to illustrate her point.

"Yes, yes, we need your names and addresses, and phone numbers. And there are dues. Did anyone tell you that?" She sat down behind a card table with a clipboard and paper on it. "I'm Diane." She looked up at us and smiled. I noticed she was slightly cross-eyed, which was emphasized by the magnification of her glasses.

"I'm Annie, and this is Bridget. How much are the dues?"

"One dollar to join, and then fifty cents at each meeting. We have refreshments, and stuff. It's really good. But on the day you join, it's only a dollar, not $1.50." She laughed suddenly, and shook her head from side to side. "I'm sorry. I'm just so excited about everything that's happening. I can barely concentrate."

"Like what?" I asked, inching closer.

"The new album in June . . ."

"What new album?" Bridget asked.

". . . the movie . . ."

"What movie?" we responded in perfect unison.

Diane glanced excitedly down at her watch.

"We know about the concert," I began. She put her hands over her mouth and suppressed a scream. "Do you have tickets?"

She nodded quickly, squeezed her eyes shut, and looked like she might need some air. "Hurry and do this, so you don't miss anything. Patty will tell you all about it."

"Who's Patty again?"

"She's the president of the fan club. This is her house."

"Oh, that's right," I said, quickly filling in the information sheet, and handing her a dollar. Bridget did the same.

"Better grab a seat," she said, as she copied our names on white paper tags. We stuck them over our hearts and walked toward the semicircle of chairs set up at the front of the room. I'm guessing there were about twenty girls, talking and laughing. They all seemed to know one another. We took the last two empty seats on the end. I was so exhilarated, my cheeks felt hot and flushed, and I wanted to make noise for absolutely no reason—just shout, and squeal, and cheer.

"A movie, an album," Bridget gushed. "These girls know everything."

"And we're right at the center of it. I wish they'd hurry and start."

We didn't have to wait long. A girl who looked about a year older than us walked to the front of the room. She had on a bright pink shift of shiny material, and her blondish hair was pulled back from her face with a thick white knit headband. She clapped her hands together several times. "Hi, everybody!"

"Hi, Patty!" the group answered.

"I am happy you could all come! There is so much to talk about, you're just not going to believe it! We have a quick order of business first. Madame Secretary—known to you as Diane Feeney—says there is now $282 dollars in our treasury." The girls clapped and murmured their approval, and Diane stood up to take a quick bow. "But today," she did a kind of turn, almost like she was dancing, "we spent $25 of it on a very special surprise." She motioned toward a middle-aged woman in a white maid's uniform who stood by the doorway in front of a tea cart. "Come on in, Vera. Come on." The woman pushed the cart to the front of the room next to Patty. "We were able to order not only the best chocolate cake ever—"

She was interrupted by a shriek from a girl at the other end of the room. "Don't spoil the surprise, Sharon!" Patty chirped.

"And . . . it was finally our turn to rent a certain something for the top of the cake." Giggles rippled through the room. Obviously they knew something I didn't. "Why don't we take off the covering and show the girls," she said to the maid.

With the awkwardness of someone trying to be careful, the woman slowly raised a large domed top off of the cake.

"I present to you—The Beatles!" Patty cried as the dome cleared the cake. Four ten-inch statues of the Beatles in their gray suits, with guitars and a drum set, decorated the top of the cake.

"Can you believe it?" Patty said. "There was a two-month waiting list. I want everybody to come up, get a good look at them, and whatever you do, don't touch. If they don't go back to the bakery in perfect condition, we'll have $100 less in our treasury."

Not a single girl held back politely; they surrounded that cake like a pack of wild dogs. We weren't fast enough, and had to look around bodies, and over shoulders to get a glimpse.

Patty clapped again. "OK everybody, take your seats. Let's get going." All the girls seemed anxious to get the meeting under way. "We have . . ." she looked up and down the row and continued, "one, two, three new members here today. Welcome." The other girls applauded politely. "We have a question we ask every new member so we can get to know them a little better." She turned to Bridget. "Who is your favorite Beatle, and why?"

Bridget blinked, and looked up at the ceiling. "I think it's Paul, but it changes." Girls actually screamed when she said this. "I like him because . . . well, he's cute, of course. But because I like the bass sound he makes. It's kind of underappreciated with all the singing and other stuff going on."

Patty nodded. "You like the bass sound. That's a new one. Interesting. How about you?" She pointed to me.

"I like George because he seems thoughtful and sensitive." The girl next to me squealed. "But really, I like them all equally because that's what makes them the Beatles, the way they fit together."

Patty laughed. "You like them all equally? No one's ever said that. How is that possible?" I didn't like her tone, so I shrugged, and kept a little smile on my face to show she didn't intimidate me.

"Where are you girls from?" she asked, as if the correct answer would be "the wrong side of the tracks."

"Santa Monica."

"Santa Monica," she repeated, "interesting." I didn't think there was anything interesting about it at all. It just gave her a chance to stare at us and make judgments. The other new member didn't wait to be asked her opinion.

"Paul is my favorite because he's the handsomest man on earth!" She slapped her hands against her cheeks, held them there, and screamed. How did the Beatles stand all this screaming, I wondered? I was already getting tired of it.

"Can I ask a question?" I asked Patty.

"Sure."

"Do any of you have tickets to the Hollywood Bowl concert?"

Patty raised her hand and wiggled her fingers. And someone else called out, "I do!" I looked down the row at the others. Every one of them, except the other new girl, had a hand in the air and was bouncing up and down on their chair.

"How did you get them?" I asked.

"Well," Patty tilted her head to the side, "my dad is the chief accountant at Capitol Records."

"Wow. Did he get them for all the girls here?"

"Uh-huh." She clasped her hands behind her back, and sort of turned from side to side. I abandoned all my pride to ask the next question.

"Can he get two more for us?"

Patty shook her head. "No. Sorry."

"Why not?"

"They're all gone."

"What if I were the President of the United States and I asked him for tickets? I bet he could get two more of them then."

"But you're not the President, so we'll never know."

"He could if he was highly motivated, right?" I felt desperate knowing she was a conduit to Beatles tickets but had no sympathy or feeling for us.

"OK, we have to move on now. I've got something I want to pass around, and then I've got a big surprise. Something I know you'll all want to see."

"What? What?" asked the other new member. I bit my tongue about her father, who could have performed a great service for mankind, if only he knew about us.

"This came to us all the way from England!" You would have thought Patty said Mars the way the girls swooned. She reached behind her and took a manila envelope off an antique secretary desk. "Something very special arrived in this envelope, but first I want you all to see the English stamp. It's got the Queen on it, and it's just super-*fab*." Patty spoke the word "fab" like she owned it.

I resisted using the words "fab" and "gear" even though I ate them like candy when they came out of the mouths of the Beatles. She handed the envelope to the girl at the other end of the line of chairs who passed it around. People exclaimed over it, and touched it like it was a piece of the true cross.

"As if that wasn't enough—" Patty paused dramatically, "this autographed photograph of the Beatles was inside." She lifted an eight-by-ten black-and-white glossy off the little desk and held it up for us to see.

It was them, all right, and there was handwriting on the top right. I felt a hunger to touch it, to grab it right out of her proprietary hands, and give it a big, wet kiss. If the din made by the others was any indication, they felt the same way.

She held it up and away from her, as if someone had tried to grab it. "I'm going to pass it around, but you may not—I stress, *may not*—hug it, or kiss it, or in any way do anything that might bend or hurt it. All agreed?"

The responses were the desperate sounds of agreement and impatience. Patty gave it to the girl at the other end of the row with a final pronouncement. "This picture will be framed and placed in the front of this room for all future meetings."

"Patty, I almost forgot to tell you," a girl from the middle of the row said. "This English shop just opened on Hollywood Boulevard, and it carries magazines that are totally about the Beatles. English ones!"

I couldn't tell from the look on her face if Patty was happy to hear about this resource or upset that she hadn't been the one to know about it first. As I debated with myself, Bridget grabbed my arm just below the elbow and squeezed tight. "Ow! Don't do that!"

"Annie," she whispered, staring straight ahead like she was frozen. "My dad!"

"Your dad what?"

"He could get those. He could order them!"

My head snapped around to look at her. "Oh, my God. I never thought of that. Are you sure?"

"No, but I bet he could. He stocks Irish and Scottish newspapers, why not English?"

"Because the Irish hate the English, and the Scots aren't too fond of them either?"

"They'll get over it if it's the Beatles, don't you think?"

"Yes," I agreed emphatically, knowing almost nothing more about it than I'd already said. "Music goes beyond borders, right?"

"Right. I wonder if Patty would let me use her phone so I could call him now."

Before I could answer, it was my turn to hold the photo. I accepted it with the tenderness and care I'd give if receiving a newborn baby in my arms. It wasn't the best picture of them I'd ever seen. It was taken in bright sunlight, John's hair was blown up on the side by the wind, Paul looked like he was in the middle of a sentence—all four were in an awkward pose. But there at the top on the right, one of the Beatles had written: "Congratulations! The Beatles."

"Shouldn't they each sign it separately?" Bridget asked, leaning over to get a good look. "I mean, signing it 'The Beatles' makes it look like their secretary did it or something."

I understood, and even agreed, but so what if it was their secretary? It was still a real photo, with real ink, in an envelope with a real English stamp. "It came from their world. That's good enough."

Bridget understood and nodded. "Yeah, you're right. Let me hold it."

I handed it to her, but it wasn't easy. I wished I could keep it forever. She gazed at it enraptured until Patty came over to her and held out her hand. She accepted it with a closed-lipped smile and slipped it carefully back into its envelope.

"Ladies!" Patty cried as the noise of talk and laughter grew louder. "Before we get into some of the things we need to talk about today, I want to show you my big surprise."

She clasped her hands in front of her. "As many of you know, my dad is just about the best dad in the whole world." The girls clapped their agreement, although until he told me that Bridget and I could get tickets like the others, I was reserving judgment.

"I want you all to follow me up to my room and see what he did for me. Last week I came home from school and . . . he'd had my bedroom covered in Beatles wallpaper!"

All the others seemed thrilled, but I sat quietly while a flash of envy burned through me. Why couldn't my dad pull strings and get us tickets? Why didn't he think of things like Beatles wallpaper? My eyes stung with the threat of tears until I remembered that my father actually listened to and appreciated the Beatles music. He was going to play some of it at a concert, even if it was on the organ. I lifted my head proudly, let go of my jealousy, and rose to join the other girls who, led by

Patty, were emptying out of the living room and heading to the stairs we'd seen in the entranceway.

"Wait," Bridget said quietly. "I need to find a bathroom." We let the other girls go ahead of us, and stood looking for something that might be a bathroom door.

"That one looks like it goes to the kitchen," I said. "Let's ask the lady who brought the cake in." We pushed open a carved-wood swinging door that led us through a pantry and into the kitchen.

The woman in the white dress stood over a pile of sandwiches, removing the crusts and then cutting them diagonally into fours. "Excuse me," I said, remembering Patty had called her Vera but not wanting to be too familiar. "Is there a bathroom we could use?"

Vera wiped her hands on a dish towel. "Let me show you," she said, and used another door that led off the back part of the kitchen. She wasn't unfriendly exactly, more like she wasn't used to people being friendly to her. We walked through a hall, out into the entryway, down another hall, and finally arrived at the bathroom.

"Wait here," Bridget instructed me, closing the door.

"Thank you," I called to Vera as she disappeared.

Bridget took her sweet time doing whatever she was doing. "Come on," I said impatiently, and when she finally emerged from the bathroom, "I want to see the Beatles wallpaper."

"Sorry, sorry." She hustled ahead of me. When we reached the bottom of the stairs, Patty and the other girls were already on the landing and heading back down. "Oh, no." Bridget rushed up the stairs toward Patty. "Can we still see it? Sorry, but I had to use the bathroom."

Patty looked mildly annoyed, but pointed behind her. "It's the one at the end on the left. Just don't touch anything."

She gave me a quick once-over look as I passed her. I smiled but thought, *What is your problem? Isn't being rich and having a powerful Daddy enough for you?* I'll bet she had her own car and real cashmere sweaters. Not that I cared.

Bridget and I walked quickly toward the bedroom. The door was open and we entered. There is no one who loves the Beatles more than me and Bridget, but both of us did a double take. The wallpaper consisted of about a thousand reproductions of photos of the Beatles in four different poses: two seated in their gray suits, and two with their band setup. Individual autographs filled up any empty space. We scanned the walls and the ceiling. "If I had to be in this room for more than five minutes, I'd be so messed up," I said.

"This is the wallpaper they use at crazy farms, huh?"

"This is the only bad Beatles thing I've ever seen."

"My eyes are sizzling or something," Bridget announced, "like when you stare at stripes."

We heard a long, high piercing scream come from downstairs. "What was that?" I asked, and we turned and headed back to the first floor.

"Maybe somebody bent the picture or something," Bridget suggested as we rushed into the living room. Patty was breathing heavily, her face splotchy and red. Everyone looked at us as we entered, but no one spoke.

"What happened?" I asked finally.

"Where is he?" Patty said, her jaw tight, her chin thrust forward.

"Where is who?"

"George. Where is George?"

"What are you talking about?" Bridget asked. I noticed that the girls had gathered around the cake. There were now only three Beatles stuck solidly in the chocolate icing. George was gone.

"How would we know?" I asked, with an edge in my voice.

"You were the only two down here. No one else could have taken him."

"We didn't steal George," I responded, "if that's what you're saying."

"Wait till my dad hears about this. You're going to be in so much trouble."

The faces of the other girls, glaring at the two of us, were tense looking, hard even. Bridget took a step toward Patty. "Are you seriously suggesting we stole one of those stupid plastic statues?" Several girls gasped, presumably at the insult to the Beatles themselves.

"I'm not suggesting it. I'm saying it."

"I think your headband is a little too tight. You better think long and hard before you accuse us," I responded.

"Who are you two, anyway? You just show up, you don't know anybody, and suddenly a valuable object is missing."

The heat was building in me, crawling up my neck to my face. "If you say one more word about me and my cousin stealing anything, I'm going to punch you in the face." I was acting like a Venice girl, and it felt good; I put my shoulders back and tossed my hair like I was getting ready for mortal combat.

"Lowlifes," she spat. "I'm going to start looking right now and see if you've taken anything else."

"We didn't take anything!" Bridget cried. "We used the bathroom."

"I'm going to call my dad. I may even call the police." She tilted her head back and started for the door just as Vera came in. "Vera, get my father on the phone. Now."

"Yes, Miss," Vera answered, but kept walking toward the cake. She took the tea towel she'd been carrying and unrolled it. Out came the statue of George, which she put back in his spot.

"Oh, my God!" one of the girls cried.

Patty turned around and saw the statue on the cake. "Where did that come from? Did anyone see them put it back?"

"I put it there, Miss Patty. It fell in the frosting. I took it to the kitchen to clean it up."

Patty looked like her head might explode. "Don't you ever do that again! Do you hear me? You scared me to death. Now get out of here!" she screamed. Vera looked humiliated.

"Why do you let her speak to you like that?" I asked Vera as she started to leave. "She's just a spoiled brat who treats everyone bad. You shouldn't let her!" Vera didn't respond, didn't even look at me, and left the room.

"Sorry," the girl next to me said softly, "I thought . . ."

"We want an apology," I demanded, staring at Patty.

"Yeah, right now," Bridget agreed.

"I don't care what you want, just leave. You've ruined our meeting." Patty looked at the other girls for support, but they looked away, sheepish and embarrassed.

"Apologize," I said with a smile, taking a few steps toward the cake.

"Better do what she says," Bridget advised, following my lead.

"Why don't you apologize for . . . for your tacky clothes, and your cheap shoes!" Patty shrieked.

"I apologize for this in advance." I scraped my index and middle fingers across the cake, pulled back my arm, and hurled a wad of frosting at the front of her shiny pink dress. Bull's-eye!

"Ahhh!" she screamed. Bridget laughed, and threw a ball of chocolate goo from the end of her fingers. It hit Patty on the cheek.

"Bye girls!" I yelled, running for the door. "See you at the concert!" Bridget was right behind me.

"The only way you'll ever see the Beatles is at Madame Tussaud's Wax Museum!" It was the last thing we heard before the door slammed behind us.

I licked the last of the frosting off my fingers. "Mmmm, pretty good. Too bad we couldn't stay for dessert."

JUNE

CHAPTER FOURTEEN

If I Fell

The only Beatles thing that happened in the next month was that I started talking on the phone regularly with Eve, the girl who mowed me down at the Hollywood Bowl. She was a tall glass of water in a desert that consisted mostly of year-end tests at school, the dreaded May procession, and a lack of any ideas or schemes to get Beatles tickets.

Eve, although still ticketless herself, had established a network of pen pals in London and Liverpool. "I write to ten girls," she told me, "and those girls mean business. When the Beatles play, they follow them from town to town, all over England and Scotland. Two girls even met John once."

I gasped. "What did they say about him?"

"They said he was nice, but kind of weird."

"Weird how?"

"I guess he says what he's thinking, and so after being nice, he told them to get lost."

"That's more like mean than weird, wouldn't you say?"

"I don't know. I wouldn't want to be them, would you?"

I'd never thought about it from the inside out. "I don't know. If everybody knows you, and you're famous and rich, and play really great music for a living, what's not to like?"

"Screaming girls, not having any privacy . . . it's probably hard to tell who your real friends are."

I was silent for a moment. "If you actually got to meet one of them, what would you say?"

"I'd tell them how much I loved their music."

"But after that, what? What would you talk about in an actual conversation?"

"I don't know," she answered thoughtfully.

"I'm sure they'd be fabulously interested in what happens to me at school!" I joked.

"And how mean your parents are."

"That's a source of endless discussion! Oh, Eve, I almost forgot. Bridget's dad owns an Irish and Scottish shop in Santa Monica."

"Cool."

"She convinced him that he should stock British newspapers and magazines because the Beatles are so popular."

"I've got a pen," she said, her tone one of utmost seriousness. "Give me the address. I'll come down tomorrow."

I laughed. "It won't be stocked until the 20th of June. He did it as a birthday present to Bridget. She has the same birthday as Paul McCartney."

After an extended silence, I said, "Eve?"

"I was just thinking, life is so unfair. I share a birthday with Chubby Checker."

"He's great, too. I loved 'The Twist,' but Bridget got lucky, that's for sure." I sighed. "Anyway, the 20th is a Saturday. Maybe you should wait to see what kind of stuff they deliver before you go there."

"Yeah, I don't want to waste a long bus ride. Call me after you see what they get, like, right away."

"OK. They're gonna sell English candy, too."

"Maybe one of the Beatles will come in to buy some when they're here, because they miss England or something."

"We'll set up a chair in the front, and you can wait there. Just in case."

"What if August comes, and we still don't have tickets?" she asked, sounding almost defeated.

"We're modern girls, we're smart. We'll figure it out."

"I'll think about those girls in England. They'd find out who had tickets and then break into their house and steal them if they had to."

"I'm hoping we don't have to go that far." An image of Patty Ewald's Beatles wallpapered bedroom flitted through my mind. Not that I would ever do anything that drastic. Yet.

The night before June 20, Bridget's dad had an accident. He and my Aunt Felicia were taking their first Irish dance class together, and someone stomped on the top of his left foot with some serious wood-heeled shoes. Bridget's mom was scheduled to take him for X rays the next day, which meant Bridget and I had to run the shop for an entire Saturday, from ten to six. My dad offered to do it, but it would have meant him missing work at Lambson's Pianos on the busiest day of the week. Not only was he their best salesman, but old Mr. Lambson depended on him to remember people's names, and what they'd purchased previously.

We tried hard not to show the adults how exciting this was for us; not just because of the feeling of independence, but because the English papers and magazines were being delivered that day. We'd have eight hours to read them, and find out what we could about the Beatles.

"You must have the store open and ready for business by ten," her father told us for the third time. He sat on the couch with his foot perched on a stool, and packed with ice. "The salesman said he'd be there at 10:30 sharp. He's bringing the display racks. I want them on the left side of the counter near the cash register. Do you understand?"

"Dad, it's easy. Don't worry," Bridget assured him. "You're in pain. Don't let this make it worse. I've worked there a bunch of times, and Annie's been there lots. We'll take care of it."

"Aye, I'm in pain, so I am."

"I'll take care of the salesmen, and setting things up, and Annie will deal with the customers." She glanced over her shoulder at me, and with a half smile asked, "Should I use an Irish accent today?"

"Only if you're sure the people themselves aren't Irish." A suppressed laugh kind of escaped through my nose.

"Don't you be snorting at me, Annie Street. I know what my customers want."

"Sorry, Uncle Thomas. I like it when you guys talk like that. It's cute."

"Cute," he scoffed. "Pay attention, the both of you. I don't want anyone getting a five finger discount just because I'm not there."

"Oh—what should we do if someone tries to steal something?" Bridget asked seriously.

"Chase them with a shillelagh! What else would you do?"

"OK, Dad. I think we'd better go. I want to make sure I've got a couple of big shillelaghs right by the door. Just in case." As she turned to leave, she gave me a look that said, *He's nuts. Let's get out of here, NOW!*

"Bye, Uncle Thomas. Good luck," I said, as I opened the front door.

"It's the luck of the Irish I've got! I'll be fine!"

As we headed for the garage to get our bikes, Bridget muttered, "Luck? With your foot two times its normal size because some clodhopper danced all over it? I don't think so."

We headed west on wide, palm-lined Marguerita Street. "Why can't he be normal?" Bridget fumed. "It's so freakish the way he thinks he's a leprechaun or something."

"He just wants to make your life richer, more interesting." I pedaled hard across 4th Street to avoid a passing Woody with surfboards sticking out the back window.

"I think people laugh at him. Did you see how Fondly and Royce looked that night when they heard him speak?"

"You mentioned Fondly!"

"Oh, that's right. I was going to forget I knew him."

We turned into the park on Ocean Avenue and headed south. The park skirted 150-foot cliffs that looked out across the Pacific. That morning was overcast, the sea a silvery gray.

"I don't understand why you're so mad," I told Bridget. "You liked him. So he chickened out and ran away for a while. He came back. You should give him another chance."

"Did I tell you he sent me a card?"

"No!"

"It was so cute. There was a baby chick on the front, all fluffy and yellow."

"What did it say?"

"That he thought about me a lot."

"So, what are you going to do?"

"Nothing."

"Bridget, that's so stupid. You like him." I turned quickly to avoid hitting an elderly couple walking on one of the park pathways.

"Bikes aren't allowed in this park!" the man yelled after us.

"I always forget," I said to Bridget, and headed for the sidewalk. She followed.

"I don't know. School's out now, and everything. What am I going to do, call him? That's so desperate."

"Send him a card."

"I don't have his address." She turned onto Wilshire Boulevard; there were just a few blocks to go.

"Thank God you weren't a pioneer, or the west would never have been discovered. Jeez, Bridget, you could find out so easy."

"How?"

"We have about a million friends in common. Ask one of them."

"Yeah, I could." We stopped at a red light. "I'm kind of embarrassed. I overreacted, huh?"

"Yes. They shouldn't have left us there, but they came back. I think you should write him."

We pulled up in front of the shop on 3rd Street, just past Arizona, next to the luggage shop. There were two young men looking in the window in tight black pants and black jackets. Their white shirts were cut down the middle by skinny black ties. Each had a large suitcase in his hand, and a cigarette in the other.

"Hi," Bridget said. "May I help you?" They turned toward us, and seemed to think we'd stopped just to talk to them.

"I'm sure you could, luv," said the dark-haired one, with a wicked smile.

I gasped, and blurted out, "You're from Liverpool!"

"A right genius you are," the other one said with a laugh, looking at me flirtatiously. "And how did you arrive at that staggering conclusion?"

Bridget got off her bike, and pulled her keys out, saying, "Because you sound just like the Beatles. Duh."

"Duh," one repeated, and laughed, as if he thought this expression priceless.

"Say, girls, what do you say we find a place to go and have a cuppa? Because my friend and I are suddenly famished."

Bridget and I looked at each other and tried not to laugh. "We can't have a cup of anything," she said.

"Ah, come on. We're supposed to meet the owner of this shop soon. We'll postpone it for a wee bit of your time."

Bridget put the key in the lock. "Actually, that's my dad you're talking about."

"Is it now, actually?" Every word and phrase seemed to have a laugh or a joke just behind it. I could have listened to them until my ears fell off. "Where is the old Dad, then?"

"We're in charge of the shop for the day," she answered, opening the glass front door, then turning the paper sign that hung there from "Closed" to "Open."

"Aren't we the lucky boys?" the fair-haired one said with a smile, and a sweeping motion of his hand, meant to usher me in. "Ladies first." They crushed their cigarettes on the pavement, and followed us into the store.

Bridget opened the front window and turned on the lights.

"I don't think we've been properly introduced," the dark-haired one said, following close behind her. "I'm Derek, and that over there is Clive." Clive nodded in our general direction as he strolled around the shop, looking curiously at everything.

"I'm Bridget, and this is my cousin Annie."

"So, Annie," Derek said, "you knew straight away we were Scousers."

"Scousers?"

"Liverpudlians." They looked like they were at least eighteen, maybe older. Just about the ages of some other Scousers I could mention.

"Do you know the Beatles?" I asked, getting right to the point.

"Aye, luv, who doesn't know the Beatles?" Derek answered with a shrug.

"No, I mean like met and talked with, not just know about."

"Of course," Clive said, walking toward us. "They played the Cavern three hundred times before they moved to London. Hard not to know them."

Bridget and I were speechless. "I don't believe you," I said bluntly.

"Test us," Clive said. "Go on, ask us something about them."

It had to be a good question, not just something anybody would know. "What was the name of the security guard at the Cavern?"

"Paddy," they said in unison. I felt a chill run through me. Not that I knew his name was Paddy, or even that there was a security guard; it was the way they said it without hesitation that made me a believer.

“Tell us something else,” Bridget demanded, staring intently at Derek. She seemed to be most interested in him, which was fine with me because the dimple on Clive’s right cheek, and his sleepy blue-green eyes, had my full attention.

“They’re very tough guys,” Clive said simply.

“Do you mean tough like bitchin’, or tough like hoodlums?”

They started giggling. “Bitchin’?” Derek repeated.

“We’re not the ones who talk funny,” Bridget said, joining in the laugh.

“I mean,” Clive said, “that . . . how would you Americans say it . . . you don’t want to *mess* with them. They’re mates, they stick together.”

Bridget pointed to their suitcases. “Are there any Beatles magazines or anything like that in there?”

“Could be,” Derek said. “Let’s have a look.” Each of them took their suitcase and swung it up on the long wooden counter. The cases were a foot wide at the bottom, made of black cloth, and opened into three parts that laid flat. On the left side were newspapers, on the right, magazines, and boxes of candy strapped down into the four sections in the middle.

We watched, entranced. Clive said, “The best of British journalism and confection stands before you.”

I ran my fingers lightly over the magazines in Clive’s open case as though they were precious jewels. “Which are the good ones?” I asked.

“That depends,” Derek answered, taking them out and laying them on the counter one by one. “There’s *Mersey Beat*, *Beatles Monthly* . . .” Bridget and I actually kind of screamed for a second at that one. “. . . *Queen*. That will give you more dirt on the Royals than you ever wanted to know. And for the more serious minded patron, *The London Times*.”

“Can we look at the Beatles magazine?” I asked, hesitantly reaching for it.

"Yes, yes, help yourself," Derek said. "Who decides which ones you're going to keep for your stock?"

"Oh," Bridget said, as if she hadn't considered that. "Well, my dad's out today, so I guess I get to decide." My cousin and I locked eyes, both as excited as if it were Christmas morning and we were the only children for miles around. "Show us everything."

Clive took out a neatly folded wire rack and began to turn it into a multileveled counter stand for periodicals. "This will give you an idea of what it will look like to your customers."

"Oh, that's so cute!" Bridget said, a copy of *People's Friend* in her hand, pointing to a cover story called, "Marmalade Making."

"That one's Scottish," Derek said, glancing around the store, "but is that the image you want to create?" Bridget listened to him attentively. "It's a fine shop, don't get me wrong. But it feels like–"

"Like it's 1945," Clive said, interrupting him.

"You think so?" Bridget kind of flinched, even though she was always making fun of it behind her dad's back. She looked around the store as though seeing it through their eyes.

"Don't people in Liverpool wear plaid wool jackets with leather elbow patches?" I asked.

"Not if they're under ninety," Clive responded.

"Or a Royal," Derek added.

"What about the kilts?" Bridget asked.

"For ceremonies or weddings, that sort of thing," Clive informed us.

"What about the women's clothes?" I asked, pointing to a rack of generously cut, dark-colored wool skirts that hit the leg a few inches above the ankle.

"You say your dad owns this shop?" Derek asked. Bridget nodded. "I don't mean to be unkind, but this is more like a fairy tale idea of Ireland or Scotland, or something from the tourist bureau."

"I like fairy tales," I offered, suddenly feeling sorry for Bridget's dad.

Clive spoke up. "You could do so much with it. Make it modern, get young people in here. Have you thought about selling records?"

"No," Bridget answered. "I didn't really know we could."

"There's fabulous music coming out of Britain now, not just the Beatles. You could make yourself the place to go for imports. They're a little different than what you get in America."

"How else could they change it?" I asked Clive.

"Dunno. Start with the mags and candy. Add the records. See who comes in, and what they want."

"And put on some music for your customers," Derek directed Bridget. She turned on the radio her dad kept behind the counter. It was tuned to a station that featured bland instrumental versions of out-of-date songs your podiatrist might play in his waiting room. She switched it to KHJ, and the Beatles version of "Money" came screaming out at us. The energy in the room increased by a factor of ten.

"We want one of everything," Bridget said, waving her arm toward their open cases.

"Hold on, darling. Let's be a bit more discriminating." That surprised me; I assumed they'd want to sell as much as possible so they'd make more money. "Let me choose the right ones for you. May I?"

A smile spread over Bridget's face and she gave Derek her consent.

"There's a whole colony of Brits here, you know," Clive said to me, as he began to load the display rack.

"In the Los Angeles area?" I asked, studying the way his hair fell over the back of his collar.

"No, right here in Santa Monica. Venice, too."

"Do you all know each other?" I asked. It was perhaps the stupidest question that ever passed my lips, but I was too focused on his translucent skin to care much.

Clive stopped and looked at me, and with a laugh said, "Are you mental? There's thousands of them. Can't know them all now, can I?"

I wanted to hand him a copy of British *Woman's Day* and say, "Read anything, just so I can listen to your accent."

"Look, Annie," Bridget said with a laugh, holding up an open magazine. "A whole article called, 'Freedom from Nervous Tension.'"

"Are you tense, luv?" Derek asked, moving just a little closer to her.

"I will be until we get Beatles tickets," she answered as she perused the article, glancing up at him with a little smile. She must have sensed something in his face, because her head snapped up, her smile gone. "Do you have tickets?"

"As a matter of fact, we do," Derek answered proudly.

"How did you get them?" I looked from Derek to Clive.

"No magic. Our mate stood in line—for a price—and bought four tickets for us."

"So . . . you're taking dates?" I hoped I didn't sound as pitiful as I felt.

Clive shook his head, stopped what he was doing, and looked straight at me. "We've been waiting for just the right opportunity to come along." I stared shamelessly into those sleepy eyes much longer than I should have. My heart pounded as I waited for one of them to say something.

"Did you know *A Hard Day's Night* is coming out next Friday?" Derek asked Bridget.

"What's that?"

"What's that? I thought you were Beatles fans!"

She stood up, tense. "We are. What is it?"

"It's the name of the new Beatles record," Clive answered. "See? You'd have known that ages ago if you sold import records."

"Oh, my God," I whispered, covering my mouth. I knew a new Beatles album was coming, but I didn't know when, and I certainly didn't know its name in advance.

"Why don't we meet in a caff on Friday," Clive said. "I'll buy the Beatles record first, and we can have a look at it over lunch. Then we can go 'round to our flat to listen to it."

"You have an apartment?" I asked, wishing I hadn't.

"You're a bit of a giggle, Annie. Did you think we live with our parents?"

"Oh, no."

"Do you live with your parents still?" Clive asked.

"When you're fifteen you don't have much of a choice."

"Fifteen?" Clive repeated, glancing up at Derek.

"I'm sixteen," Bridget said quickly, "for two days now."

"Two whole days," Derek mused.

"How old are the two of you?" I sounded a little defensive.

"Nineteen," Clive answered.

"Twenty. I'm practically an old man," Derek teased, not taking his eyes off Bridget. "What do you say? Is it a yes?"

"Yes," Bridget said, not waiting to consult me. "Where do you want to meet?"

"The Brass Bell?"

"That's a bar!" I exclaimed.

"Right. Let's meet at . . . the Broken Drum."

"You can't beat it," Clive joked, quoting its sign.

"What time?"

"Noon?"

Bridget nodded in agreement. "Done. But leave plenty of time, because you have to tell us tons more about the Cavern, and the Beatles, and what they're like."

"Bring your Beatles tickets with you," I added. "I want to see them in case I don't get to go."

"I wouldn't worry about that," Clive said softly. For the rest of the day and every minute until Friday at noon, I was filled with a kind of serenity. I really thought all my hopes, prayers, and dreams were soon to be fulfilled.

CHAPTER FIFTEEN

Tell Me Why

"Don't you dare mention their ages," Bridget whispered, just before I opened the back door to my house.

"I'm not *daft*," I said. For the last seven days, we'd incorporated every word and phrase Derek and Clive used into our everyday vocabulary. We now said *Ta* instead of thank you, *cheesed off* rather than mad, and *fizzy* when we meant soda. If it hadn't made me feel like I was going to choke, I would have started talking in that back-of-the-throat, nasally kind of way the Liverpudlians did.

"Hi, Mom," I said, as casually as possible. She and my Aunt Joyce had started their classes at UCLA two weeks earlier, and things had changed. There was tension in her face, a little edge in her voice.

"I love it!" she'd claimed several times, but classes in history, French, and anthropology were taking all her time and attention, along with her patience.

"Hi, kids," she answered vaguely, looking up from her French book, and attempting a smile.

"We're going to meet our friends now," I said, opening the refrigerator, and having a look around as though I weren't all that excited.

"Remind me." She rubbed her forehead as her eyes strayed back to her textbook.

"Just two boys from school. We're going to meet them at the Broken Drum."

"Maybe come back here and listen to the new Beatles record," Bridget said, just as we'd rehearsed.

My mom's face tensed up immediately. "Do you think you could listen at their house? I mean, if there is a parent at home?"

"Sure," I said casually, with a little shrug. "We don't want to interrupt your studying." Her body seemed to relax, probably half in relief and half in exhaustion. "Should I call you, or just come home when we're done?"

"Just be home by dinner."

"What are you making?" I asked as we headed for the living room.

"No idea."

"Don't work too hard, Mom," I called, as I closed the front door behind us. Only after we'd walked past the house next door, did we let down our guard with a sort of hug and a squeal.

"This is so totally great," Bridget said, hurrying down the street toward our rendezvous with Derek and Clive. "Now that our moms are students, and we're free for the summer, we are going to have so much fun!"

"She didn't even ask their names!" I was so happy, I almost skipped. "I usually get the third degree about every single detail."

"Do I look OK?" Bridget asked suddenly, turning around and walking backward so I could see her better.

"Fine, good. That peachy color makes you look tanner." Bridget sort of shook with excitement and smiled.

"I really like him already," she confessed. "It's like I can't stop thinking about him."

"Could you please slow down? We don't want them to see us looking too eager."

"Yeah, be cool, you're right," she said. "Do you think they're going to ask us to the Beatles concert?" It had to be the hundredth time she'd asked since Saturday.

"I think yes. At least that's how Clive made it sound."

"Tell me again what he said." I went over the few details of the two allusions he'd made to the concert.

"They haven't asked us, and they don't owe us anything. We hardly know them," I reminded myself as much as Bridget.

"If they don't, this is going to be one big bummer summer."

"We have to hide them from our parents, though. They'd never let us go out with boys that old, especially ones that almost kind of work for your dad."

"We have plenty of time before August to worry about that," Bridget responded.

When we were a half a block from the restaurant, I stopped walking. "What do we do if they don't mention it at all?"

Bridget hesitated. "We'll be bold. I'll do it. I'll say, 'So, are you going to ask us to see the Beatles, or not?'"

"No, because if they were going to ask us and then they think that's pushy, they might not ask us." We stood still, looking nervously in the direction of the restaurant. "We don't want to seem desperate . . ." I mused out loud.

"But we don't want to seem like it's not that important, either," Bridget reasoned.

". . . or that we're just using them for their tickets."

"No! I'm hoping Derek asks me out like, now, so we can be practically going steady once the concert gets here," Bridget said.

I thought of Clive's blue-green eyes. "Me, too."

"For me, or you?"

"Both."

Bridget made a little sound of excitement. "It's almost like we're closer to the Beatles because of them."

"Listen," I said, grabbing her arm as she started to go. "They're going to have the new Beatles album, and we're supposed to go to their apartment to listen to it."

"Did you think I forgot?" she asked with a laugh.

"No, but . . . they're practically men."

"They are men, Annie."

"You know what I mean. What if it turns into a giant make out party?"

"I hope!"

"Bridget! We have to be careful. They might . . . expect things."

"Let's go. Everything's going to be fine. We'll see what develops."

"OK," I answered, even though it made me feel uneasy. "We'll see what develops."

"Take it a step at a time. Lunch, Beatles talk, album time."

"Lunch, Beatles talk, album time," I repeated. In another minute we were standing at the corner of Wilshire Boulevard and 7th Street staring across the busy boulevard at the entrance to the Broken Drum. Clive and Derek were already waiting outside. They waved when they saw us, and started walking toward the traffic light to meet us at the crosswalk.

Clive was even more handsome, sexy, and grown-up than I remembered. I felt like I couldn't catch my breath. But there was something different. It was almost like he didn't look me in the eye when he said, "Hello," even though he did. Or that there was something on his mind that was bothering him.

Derek and Bridget locked in on each other and couldn't seem to get the words out fast enough. We followed them into the dimly lit restaurant and were quickly seated near the fireplace, which the owners always kept going.

I couldn't shake the feeling there was something wrong, even as we chatted and looked at the menu. Bridget and I ordered the obligatory salads all girls are expected to want; the guys ordered hamburgers and French fries.

Clive and Derek were a little like a comedy act that day, telling stories about the Beatles at the Cavern, of the girls who chased them relentlessly, of the local rival bands who looked hard for the magic the Beatles had but they couldn't find. They were funny and smart, and by my last bite of salad, I was pretty much sure I was in love with Clive.

As the waitress cleared away the last of the lunch dishes, Derek sighed, lit a cigarette, and said, "I'm going to miss all this."

"Miss what?" Bridget said, with a smile.

"American-style hamburgers and chips."

"Why would you have to miss them?" I asked, watching Derek inhale deeply and blow smoke out and up in a steady stream.

He glanced at Clive. "We've had a bit of a surprise, and . . . we're going back to Liverpool."

I stared at Clive, who couldn't quite meet my gaze.

"When?" Bridget sounded shocked and distressed.

"What's today?" he asked, although I'm sure he knew exactly.

"The 26th."

"On the 30th."

"You're going to Liverpool in four days?" Bridget repeated incredulously. "Why?"

"Our rent is due on the 1st, so the 30th seemed like a good choice." Clive tried to sound lighthearted.

"Did you know this the other day when we met you?" I asked, feeling like a fool remembering how impressed I'd been by how real and sincere they'd seemed.

"No," Derek answered, inhaling deeply again.

"Why are you leaving so suddenly? Is somebody sick?" I felt like someone had just given me a peek into a wonderful new world, and then slammed the door shut. Clive glanced sideways at Derek.

"It appears I'm going to be a father," Derek said simply. We were speechless.

I turned toward Bridget who sat motionless in shock. "Congratulations," I said softly. Derek laughed uncomfortably.

"I'm sorry," Clive said to me.

"It's OK. You're not the one who's pregnant." I cringed at my own idiotic response. What I really meant was, *Thank God it wasn't you who made that announcement*. It would have made my heart ache, crack in two even.

Derek put his arm around Clive's shoulder. "Yes, darling, thank God you're not pregnant."

"It's not funny," Bridget said, getting up from the table. "Excuse me."

"She really liked you a *lot*," I told Derek, as we watched her escape to the ladies room. He put his cigarette out with a sigh.

"And I her."

I looked at them both and made a decision. "Can we buy your Beatles tickets?" Again I felt the tension, the hidden something.

"We had to sell them," Clive said, "to pay for the fare home."

"How much did you get?" I didn't care about being too refined at this point.

"Four hundred dollars," Derek answered.

"Are you kidding? Four hundred!?" I'd been prepared to offer them $20 for each one. They would have made a sturdy profit of $11.50 on each of their four tickets.

"I noticed you didn't bring the record today, either."

Clive shook his head. "We're shipping a lot of stuff home, giving a lot away. No sense in buying it now."

"Why do *you* have to go?" I asked, thinking there was a chance maybe he wouldn't.

"I like America, love it really . . . but I belong there."

I nodded my head. "I think I'm going to go find Bridget. Thanks for lunch, guys. Have a good trip home." I got up, but instead of walking away I leaned over Clive and kissed him on the lips. I just had to know what I'd missed.

Without a word, I left to find Bridget, vowing never to let anyone win my heart so easily again.

CHAPTER SIXTEEN

Twist and Shout

After our disastrous lunch with Clive and Derek, Bridget and I went directly to the record store and bought two copies of the new album, *A Hard Day's Night,* one for each of us. "This will make me forget him," Bridget said defiantly. We left the record store, squeezing past yet another group of excited girls rushing in to buy their copies.

"Even if it just makes you stop crying, it will have been worth it." I held the thin paper bag with the precious vinyl discs close to my chest, like a protective shield.

"I should have stuck with Fondly. I know he wouldn't have made any announcement over lunch about being an unwed father." She wiped her right eye with the heel of her hand. "There, that's it. No more tears, no more Derek." She glanced at me as we hurried down 4th Street toward home. "How old do you think you have to be before you understand men?"

"First, I think you have to be a woman, not a girl."

"Do you think sixteen is more woman or girl?"

"Girl. I think by the time we're twenty, we should understand them pretty well."

"That sounds about right." Fifteen minutes later, we carefully broke the plastic seal, slipped the album out of its cover, and placed it lovingly on the turntable of Bridget's stereo. It turned out to be the greatest record ever made.

The opening chord of the first song, "A Hard Day's Night," awakened heart, brain, and nerve cells I never knew I had. I felt like I knew something, but I couldn't say what. That I could do things, that I could be things that I couldn't even articulate. I wanted to run, to jump. I felt more alive and aware than I'd ever been.

Every song was a jewel, not a throwaway in the bunch: "I Should Have Known Better," "And I Love Her," "Happy Just to Dance with You," "You Can't Do That." But when I heard "If I Fell," it reached deep, as if I'd always known the song; I understood just what they meant when they picked those chords, chose that melody, wrote those words.

We lay on the floor in Bridget's bedroom. "Make me a promise," she said, as we finished listening to our fourth full run-through of the album.

"Sure." I squinted to see if I could tell what was under her bed near the wall. A sock? A balled-up piece of paper?

"Promise you won't go to the Beatles concert without me."

I rolled over onto my back and stared up at Paul McCartney's photo just as Bridget put the needle down on "Things We Said Today," the one that started with that too tough guitar thing George did. "As if."

"No, really. Promise me."

"First of all, I won't go without you because it wouldn't be any fun. Second, if I get a ticket, it's because of something we thought up together, so you'd be getting one, too. Duh."

"I can't believe Derek and Clive were able to sell their tickets for $100 each."

"It doesn't matter. Even if they'd sold them for $50, we couldn't have bought them; $20 was my best offer, and even then I would have had to cash in that savings bond my grandmother gave me. My parents would have killed me the minute they found out."

"We fell for the accent," she said, turning toward me.

"Kind of. It's like they were Beatles substitutes or something."

"Like Coke versus Tab." She bit the nail on her left pinkie. "How are we going to get tickets?"

It was hot down there on the rug. I sat up, brushing some unidentifiable crud off my arm. "You mean if we can't buy them, or win them, or have a daddy who can get them for us?"

She nodded. "I don't know. The idea that they'll be playing at the Hollywood Bowl, while we're here in boring Santa Monica in our pajamas makes me want to throw up."

"It's a pukefest, all right. We can't let it happen."

There were three sharp knocks at the bedroom door. Bridget's father peeked in without waiting for a response. "May I have a word?" He limped into the room. His dance injury turned out to be a bad bruise, but he still couldn't walk right. "I wanted to share some good news with you."

I almost laid back down. My Uncle Thomas's idea of excitement was the arrival of a new shipment of knee socks from Scotland. "We're sold out."

"Of what?" Bridget asked, looking like she too was bracing herself against the tidal wave of excitement a shipment of socks might bring.

"Everything! The magazines were gone two days ago, I've got no newspapers left, and the only candy in the store is some I saved under the counter for your mother."

"Are you kidding!?" Bridget exclaimed. We both got to our feet, as if propelled by the news.

"No! I've never seen anything like it." He rested on the edge of Bridget's bed, rubbing the leg he'd injured, and looked up at his daughter. "It's all because of the two of you. If you hadn't suggested it, I'd still be plodding along worrying about the rent." Even though my Uncle often declared, "I pinch a penny till it screams!" I'd never heard him directly express worries about his business.

"Dad," Bridget said, sitting on the bed across from him, and leaning in eagerly, "here's what we need to do now. Stock lots of imports of English records." He looked skeptical, but interested. "We talked with the salesmen on Saturday, and they thought the shop could be like . . . like a center for all the great stuff that's coming out of England right now."

"Like the Beatles," he mused, as if it was just sinking in, and we hadn't been talking about them every day for six months.

"Especially the Beatles," I said. "I'll bet all the fan magazines went first."

"Yes," he answered, as if I were a genius. "And more people than you can imagine are coming in every day asking about them."

"They've only been in the store since Saturday. Wait till the word really spreads; you'll have to stay open at night!"

"Here's what I need from the two of you." We waited attentively. "Guidance."

"Oh, Dad, that's so sweet," Bridget cooed, leaning over awkwardly and hugging her father.

"Careful of the foot, now. This is all new to me. Maybe the two of you could help me pick out the best magazines and such, and, well, records do sound like an interesting possibility."

"Yes!" I chimed in, thrilled at the idea of getting my hands on new music. "And you should sell Beatles merchandise, like T-shirts and hats and stuff."

"Well, I . . . I don't know. Maybe you're right. Business has been very slow lately."

"There's nobody you could ask who's better than us," Bridget said. "We're the experts on all things Beatles."

"We'll have to talk to the salesmen about what's available," I said, stealing a quick look at Bridget. "Have you spoken to them about reordering, and what their other ideas are?"

He shook his head. "I spoke to one young fella, but he said he and his partner were going back to England. He said someone would come in tomorrow, and that he would be my new contact."

I refused to let visions of Clive dance in my head. "Good. But Uncle, the Beatles new album came out today. I think you could triple your business if you got Beatles and English stuff in there right away."

He glanced distractedly around the room, seeming to focus on Bridget's shamrock wallpaper. "What about my old customers?"

"They'll still be your customers," his daughter assured him, "only now you'll have more to offer them. Plus, you'd better get started on perfecting an English accent. You know, for business and stuff."

My Uncle sat up straight, and looked younger, more energetic than I'd seen him look for as long as I could remember. "Well, girls, what are you going to charge me for working on Saturdays?"

"Really?" Bridget looked thrilled. "You've never paid us before."

"It's about time, then." He got up and flinched in pain as he tried to put weight on his injured foot. "Let's start you on a weekend. How about a week from tomorrow? I should have a load of stock by then. Or earlier if the public demands it," he added, proudly.

We turned at the sound of a perfunctory knock on the open bedroom door. It was my mom with a funny look on her face. "Girls, we have visitors. I want you to come with me."

"Who?" She didn't answer my question.

"Have you seen my wife?" my Uncle Thomas asked her.

"She's at the library. She'll be home for dinner. Come on, girls."

"Thanks, Uncle Thomas," I said as I left. "Let us know when we can talk to the new salesman."

"Right, luv."

"That's good, Dad," Bridget assured him. "You're already getting into character. Keep practicing."

My mother was ten feet ahead of us, walking with a determined stride, not bothering with any friendly chitchat. It wasn't like her, I thought as we hustled out Bridget's kitchen door, across the driveway, and through our back door. Maybe this school thing was starting to take too great a toll on her, maybe . . . I looked up, still lost in my thoughts, as we entered the living room where sisters John Boss and Ignatius sat comfortably on our blue sofa. The phrase *froze in her tracks* took on brand-new meaning.

Bridget tripped over me and actually exclaimed, "Oh, my God!" before she could stop herself.

John Boss looked as cool as a prosecuting attorney who knows exactly what the witness is going to say before he even opens his mouth. Sister Ignatius looked her usual blind, deaf self.

"Sit down, girls," John Boss said benevolently, as though we were in her living room, not ours. We sat.

"Sister John of the Cross and Sister Ignatius were kind enough to make a visit to inquire about our family emergency in Santa Barbara." My mother said this stiffly, letting us know that she knew we'd told a big fat lie to the nuns.

I raised my eyebrows and sort of nodded in response, a pleasant expression on my face to conceal the horrified one I was hoping to hide beneath it. "And what did you tell her, Mother?" The future of our entire summer rested on her response. Bridget stood next to me, her eyes darting around the room as if looking for an escape hatch she'd previously overlooked.

"I told her the situation had been resolved."

I forced myself to look at John Boss, who was examining me like a dead insect she was about to pin to a cork board. Sister Ignatius blinked repeatedly, like she was trying to get huge chunks of dust out of her eyes.

"Thanks be to God," John Boss said with a quick sign of the cross. I automatically did the same, but more to protect myself from her, and because there's never a wreath of garlic around when you really need one.

"She had a question for the two of you," Mom said.

"Oh?" I felt like Anne Boleyn as she placed her head over that basket.

"Yes," John Boss said with a warm smile, regarding us both thoughtfully. "I was telling Mrs. Street that we're having a Bible study group this Saturday, and—" She waited like a well-seasoned comedian, gauging her audience carefully, adjusting her timing for full impact. "—we're going to be screening a movie called *The Robe*."

Bridget gasped softly, her left hand coming up to cover her mouth. "Not *The Robe*," I whispered, as if she'd taken out jumper cables to attach to my private parts.

"What a wonderful movie," Sister Ignatius murmured with a smile.

"Yes, so educational, so instructive," John Boss agreed. Every girl at St. Boniface knew about the horrors of this particular torture. *The Robe* was a movie made in 1953 about a Roman soldier who helped crucify Christ, and won his robe in a dice game. It's not all bad because Richard Burton plays the Roman in a kind of short leather skirt. But by the end, when he practically asks for death and walks off into the clouds with Jean Simmons, you can't wait for him to die just so the movie will be over.

A simple viewing of *The Robe* is a trick by the nuns to make you think about religion for two and a half hours. But here's what John Boss does with it. She stops the film about every five minutes for a discussion about what a particular piece of dialogue meant, or about the history of slavery, or the Roman occupation of Palestine, and makes you bring a Bible to look up scriptures to support every opinion you give. She has made a single viewing of *The Robe* last eight hours. Girls actually faint from the strain, but they are simply laid out on the floor in the back of the auditorium until they are well enough to take their seats again. It's her most refined punishment, the one she reserves for her favorite victims, her recidivists, her rebels. Those who have endured it say they are never the same afterward. One of the senior girls who sat through it three times had it on good authority that it was more painful than a lobotomy.

"I'm sorry, we're busy," I blurted out. "Can't go."

"No, can't go," Bridget added breathlessly.

"Actually, I don't think you are busy, Annie," my mother said, a definite edge in her voice. "And neither are you, Bridget." Her hand on her hip, she gave me the "You can take your medicine now or later, but you're going to take it" look. I remembered that Bridget's dad had asked us to start working at his shop a week from Saturday for real money.

"We'll take it," I said.

"Annie!" Bridget gave me a sharp elbow in the arm.

"Good. A wise decision," John Boss said, as she got to her feet. She had to pull poor old Sister Ignatius up after her. "Thank you, Mrs. Street, for your understanding."

"I understand perfectly, Sister." She escorted them to the door. I didn't even hear the complaints Bridget was hurling at me as my mom waved and watched the two black-clad women lumber down our sidewalk to their car.

My Mother shut the door tightly, spun around, and yelled at us. "If you ever forge a note from me again, I swear I will send you to boarding school! How could you do such a thing?"

"I told you why before! Because we were supposed to go to a Beatles fan club meeting that day. But you didn't care!" I raised my voice too, but not so high I'd get two sessions with *The Robe*.

"The Beatles? No, I don't care. In fact, as part of your punishment, you may not listen to the Beatles for a full month."

"You can't do that!" Bridget exclaimed. "It's too cruel."

"Oh, really? Just watch me." She started walking toward my room. We ran around the other way, through the kitchen, and got there with just enough time to close the door before she could get in. She pounded on the thin veneer barrier. "Open the door this minute!"

"No! If you touch one of my Beatles records I swear I'll . . . I'll run away from home."

"Me, too!" Bridget shouted.

I could practically feel the heat from my mother's anger seeping under the door. "Don't I have enough to worry about at home without you pulling a stunt like this?" she fumed.

"It wasn't a stunt. John Boss was being unfair. You wouldn't help us when we needed you to!"

"Yeah, otherwise we wouldn't have done it!" Bridget cried.

"You keep out of this, Bridget O'Malley. Your mother will deal with you when she gets home."

I was about to yell back when I realized this battle wasn't going to get me anywhere, and one month without hearing *A Hard Day's Night* would kill me as surely as a bullet.

"Bridget, go home," I said. "Through the window." I nodded toward the low back window we often used to crawl in and out of each other's bedrooms without our parents knowing.

"What?"

"I'll negotiate for a week without Beatles, but they're not getting *A Hard Day's Night*. Here, take my copy and put it in one of the suitcases in the hall closet; figure out a different place to hide yours."

"Got it." She pulled up the sash of the wide, screenless window, and out she went.

"Hey, Mom," I said, interrupting something she was saying that I'd missed. "I'm going to open the door." I opened it slowly and quietly. "I'm sorry."

She opened her mouth to respond, then stopped, as if my words were just sinking in. "You're sorry? Well, thank you."

She was still clearly upset, her expression pinched, her breathing a little too heavy.

"We shouldn't have done it." My admission of guilt was taking her by surprise, and calming her down quickly.

"No, you shouldn't have," she said, without too much bite. "Where's Bridget?"

"She took the window home. When you were young, wasn't there something or somebody that meant so much to you that you didn't care what kind of trouble you'd get in if you broke the rules?"

"That's not the point."

"Isn't it?"

My Mom leaned against the door jamb looking weary. "I've got a lot on my plate, Annie. I need you to do your part. I can't deal with these distractions and upsets."

I reached out my hand for hers. "I know, Mom. I'm sorry."

She drew me to her, and we hugged. "Being a parent is hard, Annie. I want you to be happy, and courageous, and curious in your life—but I also need to protect you, hold you back, make sure you don't make any mistakes."

I leaned away from her and looked into her teary blue eyes. "You can't do it, Mom. It's just not the way it works. I'll make mistakes, and do stupid stuff . . . and in two more years, I'll go away to college."

"Don't say that." She kind of laughed, and sniffed, and pulled me close to her.

"You know how you feel about school?" I asked stepping back. She nodded. "That's how I feel when I hear the Beatles."

She didn't respond, but I think she finally understood. "I've got to punish you somehow, though." Her tone was one of friendly negotiation.

"How about from now until Monday, no Beatles? That's three days." I tried to make it sound like a person who was about to be locked up in solitary for the same period of time.

"OK. And you have to clean the bathroom . . ." I started to protest but knew this was the best deal I was going to get. ". . . and the kitchen."

"You have to make sure Bridget gets the same punishment," I said. "Aunt Felicia can't give her more than you're giving me."

"I'll take care of it. Now give me a hug, and make sure those rooms are cleaned by tomorrow. Deal?"

I hugged her. "Deal." For the first time in a long time I felt my mother saw me for who I was, and didn't try to change or fix or criticize me. It made cleaning the kitchen worth it. The bathroom, well, that was strictly medicine; I just had to hold my nose and take it.

"What about *The Robe*?" I asked as she moved toward the kitchen.

"You'll be there at 9 a.m. tomorrow, just like you told Sister."

"Can't you—"

"No. That's the debt you're paying to her. If you don't do it, she'll make the next two years of your life miserable."

No argument there. John Boss knew miserable like Shakespeare knew words. Saturday, I was all hers.

CHAPTER SEVENTEEN

Any Time at All

My clever cousin hid her copy of *A Hard Day's Night* with her parents' records, tucked discreetly between *Cocktail Hour with Xavier Cugat* and *The Essential Harry Belafonte*. It was the last place they'd look. After dinner our mothers came first to my room, and emptied it of Beatles 45s and both albums. They even took our only copy of John's book, *In His Own Write*. Bridget and I witnessed and endured this violation like stoic inmates, not as sad as we would have been if our jailer moms had known about our secret Beatles listening stash. Then we all traipsed over to Bridget's room and did the same thing with her stuff.

"We've decided you can keep your record players, and play your other music until 9 a.m. Monday," my Aunt Felicia announced. "We will return your Beatles paraphernalia to you at that time." Paraphernalia? They were in full twin mode, acting as a single sort of nice, sort of uptight mental patient.

"And we expect a full report on your Saturday Bible class, and that movie," my mom added.

"*The Robe*," Bridget and I murmured in unison, like some poor Spanish peasant might once have uttered, "The Inquisition."

Here's the good news. Because we spent all of the next day in the St. Boniface auditorium with seven other girls and an ancient projector and a film that kept breaking, it was more like only one day without the Beatles. The movie ordeal lasted only about six and a half hours because John Boss had a cold, and because she thought we should "offer up" our lunch-time break for the starving children around the world. Translation: no lunch break, no lunch. We staggered out, nine silent, hungry girls, moving like zombies in the gorgeous June sunlight we'd been deprived of all day.

"Let's go to Zucky's," I whispered through parched lips.

"I don't have any money."

"Neither do I." My analytical powers had apparently deserted me.

"Do you think we can make it to my dad's store? He'd give us a dollar."

"That's enough for coffee. Let's go." We shuffled down to 3rd and Arizona, gradually gaining strength from the fresh air.

"She should just like, die or something," Bridget said, referring to John Boss.

"Why wasn't she born in Russia, where they'd really appreciate her talents?"

"Yeah, in one of those places where they have you break rocks all day."

"Don't ever say that again. John Boss might hear it and get ideas."

As we neared The Shamrock, we noticed a cluster of people standing outside the open front door. We turned to each other in fear.

"My dad! Something happened to him!" We ran the last twenty feet to the store entrance. Only then did we see that the four or five girls we'd seen were actually the end of a line that began at the cash register. Squeezing past them, we rushed up to the counter.

"Hello my darlings!" my Uncle Thomas greeted us. "Look at this, will you?" The counter was covered with albums and 45s. A middle-aged man with an English accent was talking with two teenage girls who were practically squealing every time they picked up a record.

"This is Mr. Barclay. He's taking orders for all these English records." My uncle couldn't stop smiling.

"I didn't know you had any. How did these girls know?" Bridget seemed like she was still trying to comprehend the scene in front of her.

"I didn't have any! Mr. Barclay here was showing me his wares when three girls came in looking for Beatles magazines. When they saw the records they just—went mad! I guess they called their friends, and . . ." he motioned toward the twenty or so girls in line, ". . . it's been like this ever since."

"Let me see," I said, scooting behind the counter. Bridget joined me as we introduced ourselves to Mr. Barclay.

"Oh! You're the charming girls I've heard so much about!" His mouth was packed with twice as many teeth as he needed, each one headed in a different direction.

"That's us!" I said, determined not to fall into a conversation that included the names Clive and Derek.

"Can we see?" Bridget asked, moving around to his other side.

"Help yourselves. Are you familiar with English music, girls?"

I shook my head. "Not really. Just the Beatles."

"England's pride and joy. Our biggest export since tea. Let me draw your attention to a few of our other notable pop performers." He reached for a 45 one of the girls in line seemed reluctant to hand back to him. "Thank you, luv. Just tell the gentleman there if you'd like to place an order." He nodded toward Bridget's dad, whose list of names and orders already filled a long page of ledger paper.

"This group, The Searchers, is one of the Beatles' favorite groups in all of Liverpool. Played the Cavern many a time they did. We have . . . The Mojos, marvelous group. Here's an up-and-comer. The Rolling Stones."

I studied the cover photo and flashed it at Bridget. "The blond one and the one with the big lips are cute."

"Put that one on the order list," she instructed Mr. Barclay. "I wish there was a record player here. Dad! Dad! Let's get a record player for the store!"

He stopped in the middle of taking an order, and looked at her thoughtfully. "Not a half-bad idea."

"If I may, Mr. O'Malley," Mr. Barclay said softly, leaning toward him. "Just play a little of whatever record the customer is interested in. Otherwise these girls will be in your shop listening from morning till night. No need to actually *buy* the record, if you catch my meaning."

"Ahh, yes, yes. Good advice."

The two girls Mr. Barclay had been assisting at the counter didn't seem too pleased at what they overheard, but all I could think about was the question I wanted to ask them. "Are you going to see the Beatles at the Hollywood Bowl?"

They shook their heads, and almost looked like they were ashamed. "We didn't hear about it in time," the shorter one said. "They sold out in five minutes."

"Four hours," I responded, repeating what I had heard from Eve, who seemed to know everything—except how to get tickets. Coming out from behind the counter I walked down the line of girls waiting to see Mr. Barclay's records, asking each girl if she had tickets to see the Beatles. Only one girl said yes.

"My Uncle got them somehow," she said nervously, because all the girls were listening to her answer.

"Did he stand in line at the Bowl?" I asked, trying to see if there was anything in her answer that could help me and Bridget.

"No. I don't know how he got them." Those baby blue eyes were lying like a rug.

"They're in a safety deposit box!" she exclaimed suddenly. "So don't even think about following me home!" She looked like she was scared we'd jump her or something.

"It's OK," I said, trying to reassure her. "No one's going to hurt you."

"You have no idea what it's like. Everyone hates me just because I have tickets."

Looking at the face of the girl directly behind her, all tense and squint-eyed, made me believe her. "No one hates you. We just wish it was us." In a loud voice I asked the group, "Anyone know how to get tickets?"

"No, no, no," was all I heard, in tones of resignation and despair.

After frightening the poor girl with the ticket, I went back to the counter to join Bridget. "I have an idea. Help me find a container, like a glass jar or bowl."

While she went into the little kitchen area in the back, I got a note pad and pen. I made a little sign to set in front of the green glass bowl Bridget found. "Can you help me get tickets to see the Beatles at the Hollywood Bowl? If yes, please put that information in the bowl next to this sign."

"Oh, that's brilliant!" Bridget said enthusiastically. "Somebody's bound to come in who knows how to help us. Look at all these people! The Beatles network is buzzing already about the magazines we've got. Wait till they see the records."

"Mr. Barclay," I said, "do you have Beatles merchandise? Like hats or watches, or T-shirts—stuff like that?"

He looked up from his discussion with Uncle Thomas. "It's hard just now to get much of that. If Mr. O'Malley would like me to look into it, I'd be happy to do so."

"Oh, Dad, please!" Bridget begged, putting her arm around her father's shoulder.

"Why wouldn't I?" he said with a laugh. "Look what's come of your suggestion to stock Beatles magazines!"

"Good enough, Mr. O'Malley. I'll get right on it."

"Uncle Thomas," I whispered. He turned his head, and leaned close to hear me. "Do Bridget and I have to pay full price for everything?"

He paused before answering. “The Scotsman in me says yes—”

“I thought you were Irish.”

“Scottish/Irish. They’re very close.”

“Then you’re probably English, too. England’s right next door to Ireland and Scotland.”

“Let’s not forget Wales,” he added, I guess in case something Welsh emerged, he could claim that affiliation, too.

“With all those combined, it kind of dilutes the Scottish part. So the answer would have to be, you’ll sell them to us wholesale,” I said with great seriousness.

Only when Uncle Thomas noticed Mr. Barclay was waiting to hear his answer, did he say, “Wholesale, of course. We’re family.”

“When will the records he’s ordering arrive?” I asked, turning to Mr. Barclay.

“Wednesday, I’d say. Most of them, anyway.”

Bridget closed her eyes and did a little dance.

“This is going to be such a bitchin’ summer,” I said, flipping on the radio without asking my uncle’s permission. It was still tuned to KHJ, where we’d put it the afternoon we met Clive and Derek. It shouted out the chorus of “Any Time at All,” one of the songs from *A Hard Day’s Night*.

I took it as a sign that whatever this music/magazine/Beatles convergence thing going on in The Shamrock was, it would eventually lead us to the Beatles and the Hollywood Bowl. A bitchin’ summer indeed.

JULY

CHAPTER EIGHTEEN

This Boy

July seemed to fly by. Bridget and I were at the store almost every day, even though Uncle Thomas paid us for only two of them. It was OK because the store was Beatles central, with loads of girls arriving nonstop to look at magazines, hear Beatles gossip, and buy the records of the other English groups.

Eve and her friend Mona endured a long bus ride twice a week to come in and make sure they were up on everything. Eve was still exchanging letters with girls in England who'd made chasing the Beatles a full-time job.

"Listen to this," Eve said one sweltering day in late July, pulling a letter out of her purse.

"Did you see the stamp?" Mona asked excitedly. "It's so cute! It's just so . . . English!"

I nodded, anxious to learn what Eve knew. "Who's it from?"

"Beryl, that girl in London. Her sister's boyfriend's sister works for a publicity firm who does some stuff for Brian Epstein."

"Unbelievable," I said, thinking that if I lived in England maybe I could work for a place that had the Beatles as clients. It was an angle I hadn't considered. "Read it!"

Eve looked carefully at the tissuelike pages. "There's this one part . . . OK, here it is. 'I have some information for you. *A Hard Day's Night*—the movie—will definitely be opening in America on 11th August.'"

Bridget, who was standing next to me, started jumping up and down. "Yea! Yea!"

"Wait, there's more. 'It opened in London on 6th July. Eve, you must see it. It is simply the most fabulous movie you will see in your lifetime.'" The four of us laughed from sheer excitement. "'Girls here are queuing—' That's English for standing in line," Eve explained quickly. '—hours before the movie is to begin. They come back day after day. I have seen it five times. The only word to describe it is *thrilling!*'"

I glanced quickly at a wall calendar. "It will open here in less than a month, and . . . oh, my god, the concert is exactly one month from today."

The smiles on our faces wilted. "Any luck with the suggestion box yet?" Eve asked.

"No. You can't believe how mean girls are. Last week somebody left a note that said, 'Hey, stupid. You're not going. Get used to it.'"

Bridget said, "Oh, and remember that one that said, 'Here's the number of the Tooth Fairy, and the Easter Bunny. Maybe they can help you: 679-HaHaHa!'"

"I'm taking it down," I said, reaching for the now empty bowl, and the pen and paper. "It bums me out to read that stuff."

Bridget put her hand on mine to stop me. "Don't. You never know what might happen." I shrugged, and let it go.

The shop was full, and I left the girls to help one of our older customers who wasn't all that excited about the changes at The Shamrock. "Have you got some wool hose, dear, or have you got rid of them?"

"Oh, no, they're still here. We just moved them to another place." I was leading her past the open front door just as the mailman arrived and handed me the mail. "Thank you," I said, noticing that a letter addressed to Bridget lay on the top of the pile.

"Excuse me, Mrs. Ryan," I said to my customer, "I'll be right back." She sighed as though annoyed, but Bridget had to see this. The name on the return address said B. Huxley. I rushed to the counter where Bridget was ringing up a sale. Eve and Mona were saying their good-byes and heading out the door.

"It's a letter from Fondly," I whispered, handing it to her. She finished her sale quickly, turned toward me and opened it. She read in silence, but I could see she was moved. "What does it say?" She handed it to me wordlessly. It was a poem:

Ode to Bridget

She's tall and beautiful
Hair so dark
Like the shade of an oak
Or really brown bark

I hope and I pray
That one day real soon
She'll go out with me
'Neath the silvery moon

Very Fondly,
Brad

P.S. Are you free Saturday, August 1st? I will call you this weekend to find out.

P.P.S. I hope so.

"*Very* Fondly!" we cried together.

"He really likes you," I said.

She nodded and looked like she might cry with happiness. "I know. And I really like him, too." I didn't bother to ask her if she was going to accept.

"Can I see that again?" She handed me Fondly's letter. "Oh," I sighed, rereading the postscript. "For a minute I thought he asked you out on the 11th."

"What's the . . . oh! That's the day *A Hard Day's Night* opens."

"Promise you'll go with me, OK Bridget? Even if Fondly asks you."

"Oh, God, yes—I mean, no, I won't go with him. I'll only go with you."

Bridget's dad came bustling out of the storeroom behind us carrying a large cardboard box. "Look girls! Our first shipment of Beatles caps! They're just like the one John Lennon wears on the cover of his book. Now where are those scissors?"

"Over there, Dad." Bridget pointed to a small table in the corner.

"Listen," I said, steering her away from her father, "Eve said something that gave me an idea."

"I'm listening."

"What if we moved to England . . ."

"Annie!"

". . . where the Beatles employ people. You know, like the girl Eve was talking about who worked in some kind of publicity place for Brian Epstein."

"We're not even old enough to get passports. Are we?"

"I don't know, but where there's a will there's a way, and I just don't think we're going to be able to get tickets to see the Beatles, and I feel terrible, and frightened, and if we could just get to England, things are closer together there, and we could be like those girls Eve knows who follow the Beatles from city to city, and—"

"Annie—"

"----then maybe we could see them, because there are fewer people in England, and so we'd have a better chance of getting tickets, I mean, just do the math—"

"Annie!" She said it so loud it was like having cold water thrown in my face.

I was practically panting. "What?"

She faced me and put her hands on my shoulders. "We are going to find a way to get tickets."

"But how? The concert is only a month from today, and nothing's worked so far, and—"

"I don't know how."

"Then how can you say that?" I wanted her to let go of my shoulders so I could knock my head against the wall a few times and calm down. "Because that's what you've always said to me."

I looked up into her kind, brown eyes. "That's right." I felt my breath returning.

"It's what I believe."

"But how—"

"I said I don't know. But I have faith."

"You mean like a miracle?"

She finally let go of my shoulders. "I don't know, maybe. But because of you, I know unwavering faith is the first step."

"I guess I forgot."

"That's why you have me," Bridget explained. "When one of us gets weak, the other one can be strong."

"What do you think, my girls?" Uncle Thomas turned toward us, a too-small navy blue newsboy cap on his formidable head. He looked like a train conductor on a choo choo to Crazytown.

"You look just like John Lennon," I said with a laugh.

"I thought you *were* John for a minute," Bridget agreed.

He sighed contentedly, and began unpacking his shipment of hats. "I think I'm happier now that I've discovered the Beatles."

I wanted to say, "Me too!" But as with all love, there is pain—and hurt and uncertainty. And I was just going to have to learn to live with them all.

AUGUST

CHAPTER NINETEEN

A Hard Day's Night

I closed the back door so slowly and softly you could barely hear the lock click into place. It was cold for an August morning; the sun wouldn't be up for another forty-five minutes. I hurried across the driveway and into Bridget's backyard. The light was on in her bedroom, the window open. "Bridget," I whispered, "it's me."

"Come on in," she whispered back. "Oh, wait, no. You stay there, I'll come out."

"Bring a sweater."

She grabbed a red one from her bottom drawer, turned out the light, opened the window as far as it would go, and climbed out. "Oh, my God!" she gushed. "I can't believe we're doing this!"

"Shhh. We don't want to wake anybody up. Come on."

Our white Keds sort of glowed in the dark but left no sound to betray us to our parents. We scurried down the driveway, and headed west on Marguerita. Our destination was the Criterion Theater on 3rd Street, where the very first showing of *A Hard Day's Night* was playing at 11 a.m. Our mothers had forbidden us to leave before 7 a.m. They probably wouldn't check on us until they got up, so we each left notes for them saying we'd decided to leave a "little early."

"I wore a watch," I said, touching the black and silver Timex on my left wrist to make sure it was still there.

"I've got two peanut and butter and jelly sandwiches in my purse."

"Good, that should last us." We turned and headed south on 4th Street.

"How many people do you think are there already?" I asked Bridget.

"What time is it?" I had to get within a few inches of my watch to read it.

"It's 5:12."

"I'm guessing . . . twenty," Bridget decided.

"What if there are hundreds? Let's walk faster."

"There can't be," she answered, but we both broke into an awkward slow run. Ten minutes later, we had the answer to our question. About fifty girls stood quietly in a line that already stretched to the end of the block.

"Oh, my God," I said, rushing to the back of the line. "They're worse than us."

"Or better."

"Excuse me," I said to the girl in front of us. Her dark hair was ratted out into a perfect round bouffant with the ends flipped up. "What time did you get here?"

"About five."

"Really? So . . . when do you think the girls at the beginning of the line got here?"

She pointed to a girl in a blue sweatshirt about halfway down the line. "From that girl there all the way to the first girl—they spent the night."

Bridget and I looked at each other in amazement; four more girls joined the line behind us. "Thank God we didn't listen to our parents," Bridget said with a laugh. "They wanted us to wait until seven to leave."

"You would have missed the first show," the girl said, turning away from us and cracking her gum sharply twice. She seemed to be alone and want to concentrate on waiting, and chewing her gum. Which was fine, because the five hours before the doors opened crawled by on waves of boredom, excitement, and impatience. Even Bridget and I were running out of things to talk about by the time we finally handed our one-dollar entrance fees to the cashier.

"Hurry," Bridget said urgently, running to the open theater doors in the lobby. I needed no encouragement, and we quickly found seats on the aisle about a third of the way to the screen.

The noise the girls made was incredible, as if they'd saved up their energy from their subdued vigil outside so they could unleash it here in the inner sanctum where the Beatles would soon appear. It got louder and louder until at eleven exactly, the house lights dimmed. Bridget and I joined with the other two hundred or so girls and screamed our excitement. There were no parents, nuns, or hall monitors to tell us to be quiet and act like ladies. Not that it would have mattered.

We sat for a moment in total darkness before that first, perfect, insane guitar chord from "A Hard Day's Night" filled the theater, about one hundred times louder than you could ever hear it at home. It was clear that this was an entirely new kind of movie. It was in black and white and opened with the Beatles running through a train station, chased by hundreds of kids. It seemed like somebody was holding the camera in their hands and running, too.

The movie audience screamed along with the kids on the screen, but were dead silent whenever a Beatle spoke. I was in a kind of superattentive state, memorizing every feature and facial expression, letting their voices and accents wash over me, laughing at every joke, while giving in completely to their music and their charm. Having heard the record *A Hard Day's Night* a thousand times already made it that much more enjoyable to see them play the tunes on screen.

At the end of the movie, the Beatles rush to a waiting helicopter and fly out of our lives. A girl up front yelled, "Take me with you! I wanna go, too!" I knew just how she felt.

The second the movie ended, the house lights came on, and an announcement boomed over the loud speakers. "Thank you for choosing the Criterion Theater for our premier showing of the Beatles in *A Hard Day's Night*. Our one o'clock viewing is sold out. Please leave the theater as quietly and quickly as possible so that we may accommodate our new guests. And thank you again for choosing the Criterion for your movie needs."

"I don't have any movie needs," Bridget sighed, "I have a Beatles need."

"I'm not leaving," I said, out of the side of my mouth.

"Annie, we have to . . . what do you mean?"

"I need to see it again. Now." I looked quickly around the theater; girls were just standing up, absorbed in conversations about the movie, while making their way toward the exits. "Follow me."

I headed for the side exit; most of the girls were on their way to the front exits, or the ones on each side of the screen. "Just do what I do," I told Bridget. "When we get near the side door, I'm going to step to the left and bend down to tie my shoe."

"But you're wearing slip-ons."

"Bridget!"

"OK, OK."

There were three girls in front of us engaged in excited chatter about the movie, and no one behind us. "Don't rush, just act normal. OK . . . now!" I eased over to the side and bent down to pretend to tie my shoe just as the girls ahead of us pushed the heavy door open. Bridget did the same.

"We're going to slip behind the curtain that covers this wall. Don't stand up until you're behind it." She nodded nervously.

I turned to the right, and lifted the heavy maroon curtain a few feet from the floor, just enough to scoot under. Once behind it, I leaned hard against the wall and stood on my toes so they wouldn't be visible to someone in the theater. Bridget ducked in only seconds after me.

"Stand on your toes," I whispered. "Let's move in farther." I couldn't see a thing and kept both palms touching the wall for the next fifteen feet as I led us toward the middle of the wall covered by the giant curtain.

I was just about to tell Bridget to stop, when I heard "Ow! That's my arm!" Apparently we had company.

"Sorry," I whispered. "How many of you are there?"

"Three," she said softly. "Now be quiet, or we'll all get caught."

It was stuffy behind that curtain, and more than a little claustrophobic. I distracted myself by counting to sixty five times. I guessed we would hear the footsteps and squeals of the new crowd in about that much time, which is exactly what happened.

"Bridget, squat down," I instructed. "Lift up the curtain at the bottom, get out, but don't stand up. Just slip into the nearest chair, and gradually sit up."

"OK."

A half minute later, we were making ourselves comfortable in seats not nearly as good as our last ones, but at least we hadn't been noticed by anyone.

"Do you feel guilty?" Bridget asked as the seats around us filled with exuberant girls.

"No. I can't leave the Beatles yet. I just can't. I'll put the price of the ticket in Sunday's offering at church."

"Brilliant!" she said smiling broadly. "That kind of wipes the slate clean, so no need for confession."

"Any update on Fondly?" Their date had never happened because he got sick.

"No, only that he's still got the flu."

"Did he try to reschedule?"

"Not exactly; he's still pretty sick. He mentioned something about the 22nd, but that's the night before the Beatles concert." We looked at each other for a long moment.

"We'll probably be busy deciding what to wear to the Hollywood Bowl, right?"

She smiled bravely. "Right."

The lights went out, the screams started up again, and I was transported once more to Beatleland. My resolve to see them in concert was greater than it had ever been, but for four months we'd tried everything, and nothing had worked. How were we going to make it happen with just twelve days left?

Bridget must have been thinking along similar lines because in the middle of the scene where the Beatles run around on a field while "Can't Buy Me Love" plays, she leaned toward me and whispered, "We have to be there."

All I could say in response was, "I know. I know."

CHAPTER TWENTY

Thank You Girl

"Be careful with those scissors! You're going to poke my eye out!"

Bridget stepped back to consider her work in the bathroom mirror. "Sorry. Your hair is so straight, it's kind of slippery. What do you think?" I turned my head to the right, and then to the left, examining the long bangs Bridget had just cut into my otherwise unremarkable shoulder-length hair.

"They're pretty good. I don't think they'll ever look as good as that girl's in the movie." I was trying hard to look like the pretty blond girl the Beatles flirt with on the train in *A Hard Day's Night*. "Did you ever find out her name?"

"Pattie something."

"And I got some lipstick that's almost flesh colored, and some really good black liquid eyeliner."

"We're gonna look so English! Well, you are. I'll still have my ridiculous curly hair."

"Maybe we could iron it, or straighten it or something."

"But not until after the concert, in case we screw it up. Somebody told me that if you have curly hair, you should give yourself a perm, and then the two curly things cancel each other out, and your hair goes straight."

"I thought two wrongs don't make a right."

"Are you calling my hair wrong?"

"No! No, I'm just thinking . . ." The phone rang, relieving me from digging the hole any deeper. "I'll get it!" I trotted quickly to my room, liking the ticklish feeling of the bangs across my forehead. "Hello?"

"Hi, Annie, it's me."

"Hi, Eve. I was going to—"

"I think I know where they're going to stay."

I gasped so loudly I almost choked. "Where?" I demanded. Bridget came into the room; I motioned for her to stand next to me, and tilted the receiver so we could listen at the same time.

"At the St. Pierre. I don't know where it is exactly, but we can probably find it in the phone book." A muffled scream escaped from my lips, while Bridget shook her head and spun around.

"That girl in England I told you about, Beryl, she's the one who told me."

"See? I told you we should have moved to England," I scolded Bridget. "When should we go there?"

"I guess Saturday, because the concert's Sunday." My body was twitching with excitement; Bridget was doing a little dance around the room singing, "It Won't Be Long."

"See if you can get the address, and I'll do the same. Once we're there, how will we know where to go?"

"Follow the reporters, they always know."

"What if we don't see any?"

"You will. Let's not make any specific plans to meet anywhere. Just see if you can find them, and go for it."

"You are the best, Eve!" I said, as I hung up. It was unbelievable. They were going to be in our city, breathing the air we breathed—in seven days!

Bridget lay on the bed nearest the window, stretching her arms toward the Beatles pictures on the ceiling, as though she could touch them. "How are we going to get to the hotel?" she asked.

The smile slipped right off my face. "I don't know. The bus?"

"Why don't we ask one of our moms to take us?"

"Is that a joke?"

"Not exactly."

"All they care about are their classes."

"Yeah," she agreed, with a morose tone in her voice. "If they had to take classes at St. Buttface, they wouldn't think school is so great."

"Do you know what my mom did a few days ago? She was rushing out the door and said, 'I left some breakfast for you, Annie.' I thought, oh, how sweet, she remembered I'm alive. And then in the kitchen, there's a jar of Tang and a packet of Instant Breakfast waiting for me on the counter."

Bridget wrinkled her nose. "It's like they're living on another planet. Let's just tell them the truth, and ask them for a ride."

"They've never been sympathetic to our love of the Beatles before."

"Then we've got nothing to lose."

I shrugged. "Let's get it over with, so we can start thinking of other ways to get there."

Bridget sat up and scooted to the edge of the bed, stood and stretched. "My mom said she thought being a student would make her a better mother."

"What'd you say?" I asked as we left my room.

"I said, 'Great, let me know when.'"

Our mothers were hunched over Bridget's kitchen table, with books, papers, and notebooks piled around them. "Hi," I said, leaning against the white-tile counter. "What are you doing?"

"Trying to learn enough French to pass our test on Friday. I like your bangs, by the way."

"Thanks."

"What time Friday?" Bridget asked her mom.

"Eight a.m. We'll probably have to pull an all-nighter."

My mom leaned back in her chair. "By the way, your fathers are having a 'boy's night' on Friday night, and your Aunt Felicia and I wanted to make dinner for you. Just the four of us."

"Tuna casserole!" Aunt Felicia said in a kind of a singsong voice, as if tuna casserole were a lure any sane person could not resist.

"Yum," Bridget said politely.

I was about to ask about our plans for Saturday, when my mom said, "And I have a surprise for you."

I sighed internally, but put a smile on my face. "What is it?"

The twins looked at each other conspiratorially. They probably wanted to go shopping for rosaries, or for next year's school uniform, or something equally as thrilling. "Our French professor's mother-in-law lives in Bel-Air," my mom began.

"Great," I said wanly.

"And she's been calling him all week, because there have been police everywhere in her neighborhood, and—"

"Are you free on Saturday?" her sister interrupted.

"Felicia! Don't spoil the surprise."

"What surprise?" Were we going to be dragged to tea at some old lady's house and forced to learn French?

"Our professor finally called the police himself to see what was going on."

Bridget and I exchanged a glance, the same one that we shared when her father started talking about the potato famine of 1846.

"So, what was it?"

"Some VIPs are going to be moving in next door."

"That's a fascinating story, Aunt Joyce, but there's something we wanted to—"

"Can you guess who those VIPs are?"

"Ike and Mamie Eisenhower?"

"Good guess," Aunt Felicia said, "it's pretty ritzy up there. Try again."

I was so not in the mood for a game of Twenty Questions.

"Let's see, he's a French professor, so . . . Jerry Lewis?" Bridget offered.

My mom looked at me, her expression inscrutable, and just asked, "Are you free Saturday?"

"Actually, we were hoping that you . . ." I began, but sensed I should hear more about the twins' big Saturday surprise before asking about our plans. "I guess so," I answered, glancing uneasily at Bridget.

"Good. We'll discuss the details at dinner on Friday." My Aunt Felicia let out a girlish laugh.

"The details of what?"

"Of how we're going to go to Bel-Air on Saturday to that house on St. Pierre Road . . . where the Beatles will be staying."

I screamed, Bridget screamed, I think even our moms screamed.

"Are you kidding?" I yelled.

"Oh, my God! Oh, my God!" Bridget said over and over.

"I know we haven't had much time for you girls this summer. We thought this might make up for it." My mom got up and hugged me. I didn't even realize I'd started crying till I saw the wet mark I left on her blouse. Bridget and her mom were hugging and doing an exaggerated waltz around the kitchen.

I still couldn't believe it. "Did he tell this story to the whole class?"

"No. We break into conversation groups, and he joins in each one. We're supposed to tell a story about what's going on in our lives, in French, of course. This is one he mentioned."

"What did the other people say when he said it?"

My mom sat back down, hands laced behind her head. "He didn't say it was the Beatles. I guessed. After class I asked him a question and then very casually said, 'My daughter is a huge Beatles fan. Do you think your mother-in-law could get a picture of them for her?' And he said, no, the neighbors had been asked not to do that."

"Then he realized what he'd said," Aunt Felicia jumped in, "and he made us promise not to tell anyone."

"So you're really going to help us chase the Beatles?" Bridget asked, still looking like she was in shock.

My mom nodded. "Yep. We know how much they mean to you. If you can't go to the concert, at least we can help you catch a glimpse of them."

"We might still go to the concert," Bridget responded.

"You have tickets?" her mom asked, looking surprised.

"No, but you never know."

"That's right, you never know," her mom said soothingly, but it was in the tone you'd use to calm a feverish child.

"Oh, and don't tell anyone else," my mom said in a very serious tone. Then she turned back to her studies.

I shook my head. "No, I won't, no." But I knew I'd call Eve as soon as I got back to my bedroom. We were sisters in a very peculiar army, and like soldiers, we were all for one and one for all. Beryl's omission of that one word, Road, made all the difference. We would have been at some hotel named St. Pierre while the Beatles were waiting for us to find them in Bel-Air. I couldn't wait to hear the scream that was going to come through my Princess phone in about sixty seconds.

CHAPTER TWENTY ONE

I'll Be Back

We pulled out all the stops in that last week before the concert. For a dollar an hour, we hired our twelve-year-old neighbor Leon to walk up and down in front of The Shamrock carrying a sign on a stick that read: "Need Beatles Tickets. Desperate! Will pay." And we quizzed every customer that came into the store about whether he or she had any ideas or contacts. Neither of these efforts produced results.

I called Scottie Pinkus, the manager of the Hollywood Bowl, fourteen times before I got him on the phone. When I asked if there had been any ticket cancellations for the Beatles concert, he made a sound somewhere between "Pfff" and "Shhh," and hung up on me.

Our moms lent us five dollars for an ad in the classified section of our local paper, the *Evening Outlook*. "Wanted: Beatles Tickets. $$$." We thought the dollar signs might be more effective than saying we'd pay. I mean, of course we were going to pay, we just didn't want to reveal how little we were able to pay. Our parents promised they would lend us the money for the tickets, if some miraculously appeared, as an advance against our allowance. I thought it was best not to mention that two months ago the tickets were going for one hundred dollars apiece. It was for their own protection; I didn't want the guilt of a heart attack on my conscience. But there were no miraculous tickets.

Bridget called Channel 5 to see if they were interested in doing a TV segment on the news about two Beatles fans who couldn't get tickets. They actually thought about it for an hour, but the answer was, "Sorry, kid. No go."

I swallowed my pride and called Patty Ewald, president of the disastrous Beatles fan club meeting we'd attended, to see if her dad was able to get tickets by some chance. At first she pretended not to remember me, but then she said, "Oh, you two! From Santa Monica. Not on your life! And by the way, that dress had to be dry-cleaned twice to get the frosting out. You owe me three dollars!"

"So sue me," I said, and hung up. My call to Little Miss Beatles wallpaper was an indication of our desperation. We were running out of time and ideas.

"Why don't we just ask the Beatles themselves?" Bridget said as we cleared the table after breakfast on Saturday.

"Sure, Bridget," I answered while stacking the blue and white plates, "let's just ask the Beatles. Shall we contact them by Ouija board or séance?"

"Don't be silly. I mean that when we get to the house where they're staying, we'll explain how much we love them, and how hard we've tried to get tickets, and . . . and they'll feel bad for us and give us tickets. Probably free, too."

"Are you bringing your pole vaulting equipment so you can hurl yourself over the police, and the other girls, and what I am sure is a big, strong fence?"

She grabbed the used paper napkins and balled them into a fist in her hand. "How are other girls going to know? We found out from a girl in England, all the way in Europe, about a million miles away. How many other girls could get that kind of information?"

"We got it from Eve who lives near downtown L.A. If she has it, there are others."

Bridget looked irritated. "Haven't you ever heard of the power of thinking positive?"

"You have the nerve to say that to *me*!? All I've done for the last four months is think positive, believe those tickets would find us. I . . . I'm speechless!" I wanted to throw the salt and pepper shakers in my hand right through the kitchen window.

Bridget walked toward me with her arms outstretched. "I'm sorry. It's starting to get to me, with the concert being so close and all."

I let her hug me. "Me, too. But—" I said, pulling away from her, "you never know what could happen. Maybe you've hit on a genius idea. We'll walk up to the house, knock confidently, introduce ourselves, share some conversation with one or preferably all of the Beatles, and they'll give us free tickets."

"I'm counting on it!" She laughed. "Whatever we do, no fighting. We have to stick together. If you get into their house today, you better make sure I'm right next to you!"

"I will. But it's getting late," I said, glancing up at the wall clock. "We should go. Where's my mom? I think she said she's driving." The trainlike honk from our brown Pontiac Bonneville sounded before I could finish my sentence.

"They're in the car already—let's go!" Bridget cried. We ran for our purses and were in the car in seconds.

My mom was sitting behind the wheel, folding up a map, and whistling tunelessly.

"Did you figure out how to get there?" I asked.

"Sunset to the east gate of Bel-Air, turn left, and right on St. Pierre."

"Look out, Beatles, here we come!" Aunt Felicia exclaimed, as if she was suddenly their biggest fan.

We were filled with excitement and small talk on our twenty-minute drive. I even got my mom to turn on KHJ, which was good because they talked about the Beatles almost the whole time. But there was no talk of Beatles-ticket giveaways.

I wasn't exactly sure where the east gate of Bel-Air was, but I found out soon enough when my mom tried to turn left into Bel-Air, and the road was blocked by orange sawhorse barricades.

"Oh, no," Bridget moaned. A policeman firmly waved us eastward, blowing on a shrill whistle for emphasis. There were maybe fifty girls milling around in front of the roadblock, slowing down traffic on Sunset Boulevard.

"This is it," I said softly, feeling focused and calm. "This is ground zero, we're in the Beatles zone."

"What are we going to do?" Bridget asked, distressed, looking back over her shoulder at the crowd.

"I studied the map," my mom said. "I'll go up to Beverly Glen. St. Pierre connects a little farther up."

"Won't they be guarding that, too?"

"Maybe, but there are other streets that will take us there."

Bridget and I were soothed—and, I must say, impressed—by my mother's preparation and confidence. In under three minutes, we'd parked on Beverly Glen and were walking toward St. Pierre Road. There were no guards and no barricades at the junction of the two streets.

"Oh, my God," Bridget whispered, "how can this be?"

"Act cool," I told her, "act like we live in the neighborhood." I could hear our mothers behind us, laughing and enjoying the adventure.

I'd never been on a street quite like this. Massive hedges guarded and hid many of the houses, with a glimpse available only when passing by the broad driveways. The lots seemed blocks long, at least compared to our modest houses on Marguerita. The oaks and cypresses were old, tall, and perfectly groomed.

There were no passing cars, and no problems, until we made a sharp turn. Then our Beatles dreams were temporarily interrupted. Two orange sawhorses partially blocked the road; two policemen stood on the right, talking and smoking. When they saw us, they dropped their cigarettes to the ground and squished them flat with their shiny black shoes.

"Hello, folks," the taller one said. "I'm sorry but the road's closed temporarily." They had nice faces, and gray hair, and looked even older than our moms.

"Hello, officer," my mom responded with a smile. Aunt Felicia repeated the words exactly the same way and stepped up to stand next to her twin. It was an old trick of theirs that drew attention to how amazingly identical they were.

"Hello, ladies," the shorter one said. "Anyone ever tell you you look like twins?" He laughed at his own joke, glancing at his partner. The two men stared at our moms, smiles plastered on their faces.

"Not today!" My mom kind of tilted her head to the side as she said it, and I swear to God she was flirting with them. If it hadn't been in the service of Beatlemania, I would have died right there on the spot.

"Were you hoping to see the Beatles?" one of them asked, hooking his thumbs in his belt in a kind of studied pose.

"Our girls were," Aunt Felicia said. "It looks like there are a lot of people down on Sunset hoping to get in."

"It's all under control," the other one said with a smile. "Nobody's gonna get through on our watch."

"We were just hoping to get a peek at the house," my mom said with a kind of dreamy look on her face. "We don't really expect to see the Beatles. That would be too much."

"Way too much," Aunt Felicia concurred.

The tall one who couldn't take his eyes off my mom said, "Not much to see, really. Just a big old house behind a gate."

"Really?" she said with a giggle. "What does it look like? Spanish style, or traditional . . . Cape Cod?"

He looked at his partner with a furrowed brow. "I don't know, exactly. What would you call it, Ralph?"

"I'd call it a big old house that rich people live in!" The four of them laughed, while Bridget and I strolled nonchalantly to the other side of the street. The two four-foot barricades wouldn't have stopped a lawn mower from getting through.

"How far is it from here?"

"See that tall black-iron fence? Just after this house here? That's it. Can't really see it from this angle."

"If we *promised* to be good girls, could we just step over there—" She pointed to a spot on the opposite side of the street, about fifteen feet closer to the house. "So we could see it for one second?"

The men glanced at each other, then looked behind our moms down the empty road. "Well, just for a second, I guess." The one that kept staring at my mom moved one of the barricades, which was totally unnecessary because all she had to do was walk around it.

I felt like I was watching an episode of *The Andy Griffith Show*. Officer Barney Fife seemed like he'd almost forgotten about me and Bridget he was so in love with my mom. We trailed behind them, and all six of us came to a stop about twenty-five feet from the entrance to a squarish, elegant, white Spanish-style building, set in just fifteen feet from the road and the gate.

The four adults flirted and chatted while we stared at the "Beatles house." "Are they there now?" Bridget asked one of the policemen finally.

"That's something I can't say, ma'am."

"Ma'am," I repeated with a small laugh, nudging Bridget while the cops continued to talk to our moms like they'd never seen women before.

I noticed something moving out of the corner of my eye; Bridget grabbed my arm. A black limousine coming from the other direction pulled to a halt just in front of the gate. A man inside the gate ran to open it to let the limo in.

By now the others had noticed it, too. "Is it them?" I asked breathlessly. Before anyone could answer, dozens of girls came running up the road chasing after the limo, screaming and making an ocean of noise. They must have broken through the barricades on Sunset.

The officers looked at each other in panic. "Come on!" the tall one yelled to his companion, and they went running toward the limo and the girls.

Bridget and I followed like bloodhounds on a scent, our moms right behind us. The great gate opened slowly to let the limo in, allowing girls to swarm the property. About twenty surrounded the limo, which had to pull very slowly into the parking area in front of the house so it wouldn't kill one of them.

The girls acted like they were possessed, pulling on door handles, pounding on the windows and the roof, screaming, their whole bodies shaking. We slipped in the gate on the right, not sure where to go. The two policemen we'd been talking to were yelling and trying to remove the hysterical, shrieking girls who were completely ignoring them. More girls and more police came streaming into the small area. Girls were running in every direction; policemen were in pursuit.

"Let's go this way," I said to Bridget, "around the house on the right." We ran past the limo, and as we approached a walkway that looked like it would lead us to the back of the house, we found an eight-foot wooden gate and fence barring our way. Planted inside the fence was a thicket of bamboo that looked twenty feet high.

"OK," I sighed," let's go the other way." I was actually comforted to see that our moms had stayed with us.

As we turned and hurried back to the front of the house, we saw the limo driver struggling to get out of the driver's side door. Crazed fans threw themselves into the limo the second he emerged, assuming, I'm sure, that the Beatles were inside.

When the driver tried to get the door open from the outside, he found it locked, apparently by one of the girls. He pounded on the window and said something in heavily accented English that I couldn't make out. We weren't more than ten feet from the front of the car when it abruptly and almost violently shot back in reverse at least five feet, running over the driver's left foot. His howl was even louder than the girls'. He bent over, and then sort of fell back on the ground in a sitting position. The girls inside the limousine must have realized what they'd done, because a half dozen of them slunk out of the limo like so many cockroaches scurrying away from the light.

The four of us stood in shocked silence watching the drama unfold. After the driver's foot was run over, the chaos intensified. It seemed like there were people everywhere; I even saw four girls in a tree.

Two men came out of the front door, stood on the steps, and yelled, "The Beatles are not here. I repeat, the Beatles are not here. They are in Vancouver, Canada, for a concert this evening." It seemed like there was a brief lull in activity while he spoke, but as soon as he finished, girls pushed past him and tried to open the front door, hurling themselves against it when they found it locked.

"We're getting out of here," my mom said. "Come on, stay right behind me." I wasn't about to argue; it was starting to feel scary. She walked us quickly to the left by the fence, staying as far away from the limousine as possible. In fifteen seconds, we were back on the street, just as the sound of police sirens filled the air.

"Stay calm, walk quickly," my mother instructed. We passed the barricade where we'd met and talked with the policemen and were back on Beverly Glen, our car in sight, in another half minute.

Only once inside, doors locked, did the four of us start talking and laughing all at once, scared and exhilarated by our brush with the Beatles and the police.

"Mom," I said, "if I'm ever in an emergency, or a life-and-death situation, I want you with me!"

She looked over her shoulder with a smile as she started the car. "What do you think that was?"

CHAPTER TWENTY TWO

I Should Have Known Better

Bridget heated the oil in the pan until a shimmer of heat rose above it. She poured the popcorn kernels in and shook the covered pan back and forth, making a huge racket. My job was to melt the butter in the empty pan as soon as the popcorn was done.

Our moms were in the living room waiting for us; *Bonanza* was on in five minutes. We'd enjoyed ourselves so much on our Beatles hunt that morning, that we'd planned to have popcorn and watch TV together that night.

The phone in the kitchen rang. "You want me to get it?" I asked.

"No," Bridget said. "My mom will get it in the living room." The action in the lidded pan sounded like hundreds of exploding bullets. It smelled fantastic.

Just as the last bits were popping and Bridget was about to pour it into the waiting aluminum bowl, Aunt Felicia poked her head around the kitchen door. "Telephone."

"For me?" Bridget said, looking up tensely. "I can't talk to anybody right now. Who is it?"

"I think it's that boy you went out with—Brad?"

Bridget turned off the flame and emptied the steaming popcorn into the bowl. "Can you do the butter?" she asked me, looking flushed, and a little unnerved.

"Sure."

She hustled out the door. I knew she'd take it in her room for privacy. How cool that he called, I thought. She really did seem to like him. In another minute, I was pouring the melted butter over the popcorn, salting it, grabbing napkins and bowls to carry out to the living room. "Who wants popcorn?" I said, setting it down on the low maple table in front of the TV console.

"Can I help you with the drinks?" my mom asked. "The show's about to start."

"Great," I said with a smile. But it began to fade as I noticed Bridget standing in the doorway between the hall and the living room, a stricken look on her face, phone in one hand, the receiver pressed to her chest.

"Mom," she said, "can you come here a minute?" Her distress was evident.

"What is it?" Aunt Felicia asked in a concerned tone, as she hurried to her side. Bridget turned and walked quickly back to her room, closing the door behind them.

"What's wrong?" my mother asked me.

"I have no idea. Maybe I should go see . . ."

Mom shook her head and put her hand on my arm. "She asked for her mother. Let's watch the show. They'll be out soon, I'm sure."

I wasn't sure of anything. Bridget confided very little in her mother these days, and what could it have to do with a call from Fondly? The theme music from *Bonanza* started up. We served ourselves popcorn, but our attention kept straying back to the hall. A minute later Bridget and her mom came out and stood mutely together just inside the living room.

"What's wrong?" I asked, sitting up straight, putting down my bowl.

"Nothing's wrong," my Aunt Felicia said softly. My mom got up and turned off the TV.

"Did something happen to Fondly?" I was suddenly alarmed by the look on Bridget's face, and the smudged mascara on her cheeks. "Why are you crying?" Bridget was tough; she almost never cried.

"Bridget wants to talk to you about something." Why was her mother doing all the talking? I stood up slowly, with a growing fear in me.

"What is it?" As I walked toward Bridget, she turned and went back to her room. Closing the door behind us, she sat down heavily on the edge of "Paul's bed" and stared at the carpet. "If you don't tell me what's going on, I'm going to explode," I said.

"Remember what happened today at the Beatles house?"

"A lot of stuff happened at the Beatles house. Which part?"

"When the driver had his foot run over."

"Of course I remember." Bridget was having trouble looking me in the eye.

"Well . . . it turns out Brad's dad owns a limousine service."

"And?"

"He owns the limousine we saw. That driver works for Brad's dad."

"Why are you suddenly calling Fondly Brad?"

"That's his name, and I don't want to accidentally call him Fondly."

"OK, but . . . would you just get to the point?"

"Part of the man's foot is broken. I guess he's from the Philippines, or somewhere like that."

"And?" I made a motion with my hands to indicate she should get this story rolling at a faster pace.

"He's sort of blackmailing Brad's father. He wants a ticket back to the Philippines and a month's pay without working."

"Fascinating, but what has this got to do with you, and why are you so upset you're crying? You didn't even cry when my mom smashed your fingers in the car door."

She squirmed uncomfortably on the bed. Then, breathing deeply, it all came out in a rush of words. "The Beatles people gave the man two tickets to the concert tomorrow to say they're sorry, and not get sued, but the driver doesn't care about the Beatles, and has no family here, and so he gave them to Brad's dad as part of the deal—"

I inhaled slowly, deeply, like someone in a closed coffin as I understood what she was trying to tell me.

"—and so Brad asked me to go with him to the Beatles concert, and his dad is going to give us a limo and everything." She cringed as she waited for my response, like a child might wait for a nun's ruler to come crashing down on her knuckles.

Everything inside me felt like it melted and was seeping out onto the floor. My lips trembled, the corners of my mouth pulled downward, my eyes ached as tears pooled behind them, ready for a possible torrent.

"That's great," I managed, not sure where to look. "You should go. It will be great." I willed myself to stand, but my legs wouldn't respond.

"I'm sorry!" she cried. "It's not my fault."

"It's OK," I whispered.

"What would you do?"

My shoulders trembled in a kind of shrug, my lips moved, but no words came. "Do you want me to say 'No, I won't go'? I will, I really will."

I looked up at Bridget, blurry now as seen through my tears, and saw that she looked almost as distraught as I felt. "No. Of course not. You have to go." I was breathing hard as I spoke. In thirty more seconds, I would be sobbing. "Congratulations. I think I better go." I ran out of her room, across the driveway, and through the back door of our kitchen.

My dad and Bridget's dad were standing by the sink, each with a beer in hand, getting ready to go bowling. "Hi, honey!" my dad said, before he noticed my face had collapsed. "What's wrong?" I ran for my room. "Annie! What's wrong?"

I locked the door and fell face down on my bed, burying my head in my pillow, letting all my tears, my sadness, my disappointment, my jealousy, my anger pour out. I didn't care who heard me or what they thought. I had tried my hardest and failed to achieve the one thing that was most important to me. Luck had graced Bridget, not me. It's not that I begrudged her that luck, I just couldn't figure out why I couldn't have some, too.

"What's wrong with me?" I asked myself over and over again. "What's wrong with me?" *What's the point in even living,* I wondered, *if you're just a big loser, and always will be.*

I lay there until there were no tears left, and fell asleep on the damp pillow.

CHAPTER TWENTY THREE

From Me to You

"Annie? It's me, honey. Open the door."

"It's OK, Dad. I'm fine." I glanced at the clock; it was almost 9:30. My bedroom was lit only by the tiny lamp on my desk.

"Please, Annie, just open the door."

I sat up, a little disoriented. "All right," I said, not even sure he heard me, and shuffled slowly to the door.

"Hi, Dad." It took me a few seconds before I could even look up at him. I was afraid I would start crying again because he'd have some pitiful "I feel so bad for you" look on his face.

"Do you remember when you were a kid, Annie—"

"Nothing before I was about four," I answered, attempting some humor, appreciating his concern, but kind of wishing he'd go away.

"—and you'd leave your bedroom door open, and I'd play 'Claire de Lune' on the organ to put you to sleep?"

I nodded, wishing I was a kid again, instead of the loser teen I so clearly was. "I'd like to do that for you tonight." The tears poured out of my eyes, and I hugged my dad until I stopped crying.

"You let me know when you're ready." That had been our routine when I was little. I'd get cozy in bed with all the right blankets and stuffed animals and yell, "OK, Dad!" and he'd begin to play.

I sniffed and nodded. “Thanks, Dad. I love you.”

As I turned away to get ready he said, “I have a surprise, too.”

“Great.” I was too tired and depressed to even guess what the surprise was. “Goodnight. I’ll be ready in a minute.” Not long after that, I turned out the last light and yelled, “OK, Dad!”

The first heartbreaking notes and chords of “Claire de Lune” sounded. After a wave of sadness, the music always comforted me. I could see the moon in my mind’s eye, sometimes half-covered with dark, rushing clouds, sometimes rising full over a still lake. By the time he was finished, I was calm, my mind at rest, my troubles on hold till the morning.

Then came his surprise. He began to play “If I Fell.” It had never sounded more tender, more vulnerable, even when the Beatles sang it. I lay on my back overwhelmed by my dad’s ability to understand a song, to get inside it, to make it his own.

I got out of bed, threw a robe over me, and walked barefoot into the living room, where he sat at the organ, eyes closed, lost in the music. I slid onto the bench next to him, and put my arm around his waist. The last notes faded into the night. “I’d like to go with you tomorrow and hear you play,” I said.

“To the El Capitan? Really?” He sounded so surprised and touched, that I felt kind of bad, like he’d waited a long time to hear me say those words.

I leaned against him for a second. “Really. That was so beautiful.”

“I have a whole Beatles medley I play now.”

I laughed softly. “Don’t tell me which songs you’ve learned. I want to be surprised.”

“Goodnight, Annie,” he said, kissing my temple.

“Goodnight, Dad. And thanks.” “Claire de Lune” echoed in my heart and intertwined with “If I Fell” like the world’s most beautiful lullaby until I fell asleep.

CHAPTER TWENTY FOUR

I'm Happy Just to Dance With You

I thought about going over to see Bridget before we left for the El Capitan, but I didn't want to risk falling back into my dark hole of self-pity. Besides, between eight o'clock mass and a quick breakfast afterward, we barely got out by 9:30, the latest we could leave for the eleven o'clock performance. My dad played for almost an hour and a half straight, so he had lots of last-minute details to attend to once we arrived.

"Is it OK if I wear these, Dad?" I pulled his sunglasses out of the glove compartment, as he backed the station wagon out of the driveway.

He hesitated briefly before saying, "Sure. Just put them back in the case when you're done." Not only did they hide what I was sure were the puffiest post–crying jag eyes ever, they also made me feel a little mysterious, like a woman with a secret, or a past, or a broken heart. I kept them on even after we entered the theater.

The El Capitan showed movies seven days a week, but in honor of its history as one of the great theaters that opened before "talkies" existed, it had theater-organ concerts every Sunday. There were usually about twenty-five people in the audience. "It's an acquired taste," my dad used to say, without the least bit of irony. They tended to be either older people who'd grown up when silent movies were accompanied by live organ, or musicians who actually liked the organ and appreciated the skill required to play it well. I was simply a grateful daughter who took her seat almost halfway back from the stage, because it meant no one was near me, and if by any chance my tears reappeared, no one would see me cry.

The concert began precisely at eleven with an announcement. "Good morning, ladies and gentlemen, and welcome to the El Capitan Theater. With us this morning is Mr. James Street on the Mighty Wurlitzer organ, playing your favorites from yesterday and today. We hope you enjoy our presentation."

The lights slowly dimmed. A spotlight shone into the darkness of the orchestra pit in front of the stage. Then through the magic of stage craft and hydraulics, the Mighty Wurlitzer, and my dad, rose up out of the pit, lifted gracefully to stage level. The four-keyboard wonder looked like a golden chariot; the pop and swing of "In the Mood" poured out of it, filling the room like the voice of God. My dad looked to the left, and then to the right, nodding and smiling, and acknowledging the applause at his dramatic entrance.

He always opened with Glenn Miller's "In the Mood." He said it made people feel good, loosened them up, made them glad they had come. Plus, it gave him a chance to show off a little with all those little rhythmic bounces and brass sounds.

Then came some kind of insane Brazilian song called "Tico Tico." You practically expected a conga line to come kicking across the stage and down into the aisles. Just as he was getting into it, I saw a light from an exit door not too far from me being opened. I glanced over my shoulder. It looked like four or five not-too-quiet people trying to slip into the very back row. They were maybe a dozen rows behind me. My attention went back to my dad as "Tico Tico" rose to its climactic conclusion, and his hands flew up in a flourish at the end.

The small audience applauded enthusiastically. The newcomers in the back row even yelled "Bravo." They were talking and making a ton of noise. It sounded like a bunch of guys, kind of out of character for one of my dad's shows.

He was really revved-up now. I could see it in his body language—shoulders and head held high, poised, expressing his joy, arms and fingers flying from one keyboard to the next. When he played the third song, the theme from "Peter Gunn," the guys in the back clapped, hollered appreciatively, and laughed. They were starting to get on my nerves. I turned around, lowered my dark glasses, stared at them for a few seconds, and then turned back around. The idea that they might be mocking my dad was starting to take hold of me. No one was going to make fun of my dad, not while I was around.

A few seconds later, I smelled cigarette smoke, and knew exactly where it was coming from. I didn't think they even let people smoke in theaters anymore, but I wasn't sure; otherwise I would have asked them to put it out.

They talked and laughed softly till "Peter Gunn" ended, then applauded and cheered loudly. By then I was so annoyed with them, they were all I could think about. Why didn't they act more respectfully? This was a concert, not a ball game. That was my dad down there, not some nobody.

My dad looked to each side of him at the end of the song, smiled, nodding his thanks to the audience for their response. He paused and waited for quiet before he began his next piece. I had a feeling it would be his Beatles medley, and I was right. It began with the song he'd played me last night, "If I Fell." The guys in back of me just went crazy, acting like they couldn't believe what they were hearing, and talking and laughing louder than ever. A few other people in the audience even turned around. "Yes, it's a Beatles song," I wanted to yell at them. "Now quiet down and listen. Try to appreciate it . . . if you can!"

The last sweet chords repeated at the end of the song, slow and heartfelt. Then my dad, almost by magic, made that chord be the first chord of the next song, "I'm Happy Just to Dance with You." You'd have thought those guys were bigger Beatles fans than me and Bridget the way they carried on. They were practically talking at a conversational volume, laughing, and there was that cigarette smoke again.

My poor dad. He worked so hard on his songs, he practiced hour after hour, and he had to put up with people acting like they were in a bar listening to a jukebox. I whipped off my sunglasses, turned around fast, scowled at them, and turned back towards my dad, hoping my message had been clearly communicated. I heard some giggles, and they seemed to quiet down a little, until my dad began the third song of the medley, "This Boy."

"Oh, God!" one of them exclaimed. "I can't believe this!" Then, two of them actually started singing along. That's it, I thought, they don't get to do this to my dad. I rose from my seat and ran up the steps to the back row, where the four of them were sitting. I still had my sunglasses on, which made it hard to see, but I hoped it gave me some little edge of toughness. They stared at me as I approached them.

"Excuse me!" I said in as loud a whisper as I dared. "That's my Dad." I pointed back toward the organ. "He's worked very hard to learn this music. Please show him the respect he deserves for being the great musician he is!"

"But that's what we were doing," one of them said.

"Sorry if we upset you, miss. We think he's fab."

"And you can drop the fake Liverpool accents. I know what real Scousers sound like," I said, thinking of Clive and Derek. The four of them bent over, covering their mouths to quiet their laughter.

I yanked my sunglasses off, ready to really give it to them like John Boss would have.

"How do *you* know about Scousers, then?"

I looked, I stared, I leaned forward to get a better look, and then my mouth fell open. It was George Harrison speaking to me. Real, live, in-person, smiling, and waiting for me to answer him.

"I, I—" Ringo Starr was sitting next to him. The two men next to Ringo I didn't recognize.

"You say that's your father?" Ringo whispered.

I nodded my head.

"We used to go up to Manchester every week to hear the Mighty Wurlitzer. We meant no disrespect."

"Move over, Ringo," George said. "Join us." He motioned with his hand for me to sit down in the seat Ringo had just vacated. I actually had to kind of climb over George's legs to get to the empty seat. I sat down in a total state of shock, and looked first at George, and then at Ringo, to make sure it was real.

"He's great, your dad is," George said softly, tilting his head just a little toward me.

One of the two men I didn't recognize leaned over and said quietly, "Sorry about the racket. Your dad's a bit of all right."

"Thanks," I answered, using the chance to steal another look at Ringo. He caught me, smiled, put his finger to his lips and said, "Shhh." I laughed.

I felt a tap on my left shoulder. "How did your dad know about the Beatles?" George asked.

"From me. I play your music all the time." His eyebrows went up as if to say, *Oh, really?*

"Are you coming tonight, then?"

"I couldn't get tickets. I tried everything."

George leaned over me, and called out to the man on the end. "Neil, can you get her tickets?"

"How many?" he responded. George looked at me.

"Would four be too many?"

"Four," he said to Neil, who took a pad of paper out of his pocket and wrote something down.

"Call this number after two," he said softly. "They'll tell you everything you need to know." I had to reach across Ringo to get the paper, and brushed against his leg. I thought the paper would fall right out of my hand, but I managed to hang on to it. I slipped it into a compartment in my purse, and zipped it shut.

"Thank you," I told George. "You have no idea how much this means to me."

"Tell your dad how much we enjoyed him." I nodded and started to get up.

"We can only stay for another song," George said. "You don't have to go."

We were all quiet as "This Boy" ended. They applauded and yelled as loudly as they had before I came to tell them it was too much. My dad's next song was a Latin number I didn't recognize. Halfway through it, Ringo looked at his watch and then around me at George.

George noticed. "Time to go?" he asked.

Ringo nodded and made a face like he didn't want to, but it was time. We all got up, and filed out into the wide aisle.

"Do you have a camera?" George asked.

"No."

"Mal, do you have your camera with you?"

"Yeah," Mal answered, digging into a leather satchel he held.

"Take a picture for . . ."

"Annie. Annie Street."

"For Annie Street."

After positioning myself between George and Ringo, Mal said, "One, two, three," and a big flash went off. Now it was me who didn't care how much we were disturbing the other patrons. Shame on me!

George held his hand out. "Nice to meet you, Annie Street," and turned quickly away.

Ringo did the same but gave me a peck on the cheek. I think I must have said, "Thank you so much, I'm so glad to meet you," about a thousand times.

Mal, who was tall and seemed very sweet, held a notebook and pen out for me. "Put your address there, and I'll get one to you."

"Really?" I struggled to write my own address correctly.

"Bye, luv," he said. The others were already gone. He rushed to catch up as the side door closed.

I sat down first in the seat George had occupied, feeling his presence, trying to smell him and remember every word he said. Then I did the same in Ringo's chair, and remembered he'd *KISSED!* me, however fleetingly. I almost fell down between the rows.

Finally, back in George's seat, I listened to the rest of my dad's concert, having gone from being the saddest girl in the world to the happiest girl in the world in one brief hour.

CHAPTER TWENTY FIVE

I'll Follow the Sun

On our drive home, I almost didn't tell my dad what had happened. I was afraid he wouldn't believe me, and my parents would have me hauled off to the funny farm before I could see the concert.

First I told him how great he played, and how wonderful his song choices were, especially the Beatles medley. "Oh, boy," he said excitedly, "there were some people near the back who really seemed to enjoy it. That makes it so much better for me."

Only then, when we were almost home, did I say, "Something kind of interesting happened when you were playing."

He listened quietly, and as we pulled into the driveway he said, "Are you sure it was them, Annie?"

I stopped myself from laughing, and said simply, "Yeah, dad, I'm sure." He examined the piece of paper Neil had given me with the number to call after two o'clock.

"Do you mind if I make the call?" he asked. Part of me did mind, because in my teenage fantasy, George would answer the phone, remember how beautiful and fab I was, and ask me out on a date.

"That would be OK," I answered, assuming the Beatles had people to take care of last-minute things like our tickets.

At exactly two, I stood next to my dad as he dialed the number from our phone in the kitchen. "Yes, this is Jim Street, Annie Street's father. We were given this number to call about four tickets to the concert tonight that have been reserved for us." After a few seconds, a look of surprise and pleasure washed over his face. "Sure, that's great: Go to Will Call by seven. Not a problem. Thanks so much." He looked at me with eyes shining, as if he was just that moment believing my story—and understanding the enormity of what had just happened.

"Who are you going to ask to go with you?" he asked, after telling me the details of his short phone call.

"I'd like you to go. Without you, this wouldn't have happened."

"Oh . . . are you sure, Annie? I'm an old guy, and—"

"Yes, Dad, you for sure. And I don't want to hurt Mom's feelings, but I want to ask my friend Eve and her friend Mona. They're huge fans like me and Bridget, and this will be like the best thing that ever happened to them in their whole lives."

He glanced at the clock. "We should leave no later than 5:30. Are we going to be giving your friends a ride?"

"I don't know yet. If we do, we have to leave really, really soon, like almost now, because they live near downtown."

He nodded quietly. "I'll ask your mother to make some sandwiches. You change, call your friends, and we'll plan to leave by three. Maybe you should bring a book in case you get bored waiting."

I laughed, and hugged him quickly. "Bored is the one thing I won't be tonight."

I ran to my bedroom to call Eve. "Eve, are you busy tonight?" I asked innocently.

"Don't ask me to do some stupid thing that's supposed to take my mind off the fact that I'm not at the concert, because it won't work."

"I think I have just the thing you need—four tickets to the Hollywood Bowl!"

There was silence on the other end of the line. "Eve?"

In a choked voice she said, "If you're teasing me, I swear to God I'll—"

"It's no joke, Eve. It's a miracle!" I told her briefly what had happened, at least during the pauses between her screams of excitement and amazement.

"You need to call Mona, and I need to get ready," I told her finally, realizing it was almost 2:30.

"What about Bridget?" Eve asked just before we hung up.

"She'll be there, too," was all I said. There would be plenty of time later to tell her about Bridget and Fondly. I mean, Brad. I needed to start calling him Brad, too.

"I have to do one last thing," I said to my dad as I raced out the door and over to Bridget's house. I knocked on her bedroom door; I could hear her singing along to "You Can't Do That."

"Come in!" When she saw me, she kind of froze. "Oh, Annie, I'm so sorry," she said.

"I'm sorry, too. You didn't do anything wrong." We hugged, and as I sat down on "John's bed" I said, "Promise you won't get mad at me if I tell you something?"

"Of course! God. Tell me, what?"

She didn't get mad, but she practically threw herself on the ground with envy and excitement when I told her about meeting George and Ringo. "And they like *organ* music..." she said, mystified, kind of shaking her head. "Oh, well, I still like them. The important thing is, we're both going to the concert! I didn't think I was going to be able to enjoy it very much without you there."

"Thanks." It was about the nicest thing in the whole world she could have said.

CHAPTER TWENTY SIX

She Loves You

I think my dad was almost as excited as we were when we pulled into the long line of cars waiting to get into the Hollywood Bowl parking lot. Hoards of girls walked, ran, and practically flew past us.

It was a warm August night, with a cool ocean breeze floating in from the west. It wouldn't even be dark yet when the Beatles played, if they went on at eight like they were supposed to.

I sat in the back seat of our blue station wagon, behind my dad. *If it hadn't been for his love of music, we wouldn't be here,* I thought. But what was the lesson for me in all that I'd experienced in the four months since Bridget told me about the Beatles concert? I wasn't sure. I'd tried my hardest, and failed to get tickets. Then they came out of nowhere. "They didn't come out of nowhere," a voice inside me said. "They came because you were in the right place, doing the right thing, for the right reasons." It was more than my fifteen-year-old brain could comprehend. All I knew was that whatever else happened to me in my life, I would remember this night and every single thing that led up to it.

"Annie?" Eve said, turning around to look at me from the front passenger's seat. "Are there any other details you forgot to tell us about when you met them?"

I shook my head and smiled. "No." The truth was, I didn't mention the photo Mal took. The chances of that photograph ever showing up on my doorstep were slim to none. I decided that the gift I'd received was plenty big, and to ask for anything else would be greedy.

"Here we go!" my dad said as we entered the parking structure. The three of us exploded with excitement, with gratitude that luck had found us, or God had blessed us, or whatever you wanted to call it—positive thinking, faith, determination, fate, remembering anything can happen.

I hadn't heard a single note yet, but I knew this would be the best concert of my life.

***

On October 1, a manila envelope arrived with three stamps on it, three little Queen's heads all in a row. I opened it carefully with a letter opener, and slowly pulled out a black-and white eight-by-ten photograph. There we were—George, Annie, and Ringo—each of us with our own goofy smile. George's arm was over my shoulder, Ringo's around my waist. There was no note or letter with the photo.

I stared at it like the miracle it was, knowing I would show it only to Bridget, and my parents. It was private, to be treasured, used for gratitude, not showing off. Well . . . maybe just for a minute.

"Bridget!" I screamed, running out the kitchen door to her house. "Bridget, I have something to show you you're not going to believe!"

***

Coda

None of my fellow fliers seemed to mind that I'd laughed out loud and cried unashamedly several times as I devoured the typewritten copy of *Chasing the Beatles* on the way to Chicago. I'd gone into another time and place, one full of innocence, pain, and wonder. And fun—sheer live-every-moment-like-it's-your-last *fun*. The second I was off the plane, I dialed Bridget's cell number.

"Annie, you're here!" she cried. "How was the flight?"

"Fine, Bridg, fine." I began walking faster at the sound of her voice, trying to keep an eye on the signs that would lead me to car rentals. "Remember how you asked me to bring you something?"

"Yes! Can you tell me, or is it a surprise?"

"It's a surprise. Besides, you'd never guess in a million years."

"You brought the cure for cancer with you! Oh Annie, how thoughtful." She laughed.

"Maybe, maybe not. But it's strong medicine, and very, very healing."

She exhaled loudly. "How soon can you get here?"

"Another half hour, more or less. I didn't check a bag."

It was then that I heard the longing in her voice, along with the fear and the hope. "I can wait. Better hurry, though."

Her voice broke as she choked a laugh through her tears. “My hair started falling out this morning. It could be all gone by then.”

I broke into a run. “Hold on Bridget. I’m coming. I’m on my way.”

And I’m bringing the Beatles with me.

Acknowledgments

Thanks to all the grown-up girls who remembered for sharing their Beatles stories with me. Whether you jumped in the pool on St. Pierre Road, broke through the barricades, or waited for months to rent those Beatles figurines for the cakes at your Beatle parties, I salute you.

Thanks to my mom for driving her girls around Brentwood and beyond to catch a glimpse of their heroes.

A huge thank you to my dad who managed to get tickets to send three of his homesick girls to see the Beatles at the Hollywood Bowl.

Thanks to Greg Pitzer, Eileen McNally, Arthur Barrow, Cindy Pitzer Howard, and Susan Pitzer for reading the manuscript and encouraging me.

A special thanks to Cindy Pitzer Howard for letting me use "Fondly."

Thank you to Margery Schwartz for her excellent editorial assistance, and for liking what she read.

And lastly, thanks to the Beatles, for cracking our hearts open, and changing our lives forever.

Made in the USA
San Bernardino, CA
17 April 2014